M'LORD O' THE
WHITE ROAD

M'LORD O' THE WHITE ROAD

BY

CEDRIC FRASER

WILDSIDE PRESS

CONTENTS

Contents

CONCERNING CERTAIN TRAVELERS AND
A SLEEPY MAN

THE wind howled round the gable of "Ye Olde
Whyte Hart."

It moaned away into the distance, then, with
a swirling shriek, it caught up the heavy drops
of rain and dashed them viciously against the
tiny window panes of the Inn.

It rattled the great bolts of the taproom door,
and slipping in beneath it blew away the sawdust
in a wide semicircle.

It whistled with a hollow roar across the chim-
ney top, and every now and then a down-sweeping
gust puffed a soft filmy cloud of smoke across the
wide hearth into the oak paneled room, accentu-
ating the dimness of the light from its guttering
candles.

"Ugh," grunted one of the men sitting before
the blazing log fire. " 'Tis a blackguardly night,
Benjamin. A plaguy night in very truth, my
little fat friend."

He was a tall, loose-limbed fellow with small

1

piercing eyes and thin hawkish face. A white
scar ran from the tip of his nose to the top of
his left cheek bone. A dilapidated wig was
perched upon his bullet-shaped head, and long
riding boots hung limply about his lean shanks.

He bent forward and turned over his great
riding coat, which hung steaming across the back
of a chair the better that it might dry before the
blaze; then he leaned back once more, and, lifting
his muddy feet on to the small table beside him,
balanced himself on the back legs of his chair.
This done, he proceeded leisurely to fill his long
clay pipe.

There were only three other men in the taproom. One was a yokel who lounged against the
bar, gaping stolidly into his big mug of foaming ale. He was dressed in smock and gaiters,
with an old felt sun hat pulled well down over
his rough red hair. Every time the wind whistled
round the inn, he tugged his hat tighter on his
head and with each patter of the rain upon the
panes, he spat into the sawdust on the floor.

The second occupant was asleep in the far corner, one of his legs on the form upon which he
sat, the other thrust well into the room. His back
was half against the paneled wall and half
against the window. His head hung forward on

his breast, his chin and nose hidden within his folded arms.

Excepting that he was a man long of limb and big of bone, it would have been hard to describe him. There was his hat though, perched on the back of his head, that bespoke him as a traveler, since it was tall and furry, such as was more often seen in the Mall of London than in the taproom of a Kentish wayside inn, half a mile from the village of Sevenoaks.

The third man was obviously the companion of him who had cursed the weather. He was a stout little fellow, so burly indeed as to appear unusually squat. 'Twas plain that when he stood up, the skirts of his riding coat would almost trail upon the ground, and since his boots were too long for him, he had perforce to keep his legs stretched stiff, since he could not bend his knees. His face was as round as his body, and his eyes twinkled merrily in the firelight.

He was holding a huge pot of ale in his left hand, balancing it—between copious draughts— on his ample paunch. His right hand hung loosely upon a large pistol butt protruding from his crimson sash. He looked, indeed, a very merry man, with a mighty stern purpose before him.

"A dirty night say you, Simon," he called

blithely, "and why miscall the night. I'll warrant that many such a night hath brought blessings from your big mouth ere now. True, the
wind doth howl, but noise ne'er hurt any one.
True, the bolts do rattle, but bolts are made to
rattle, Simon, and by their rattle do they proclaim themselves as bolts to all who pass this
inn, including any chance marauder who, hearing their rattle, needs must know the door is
bolted, and thereby deem it worthless to expend
his energy upon it."

Simon shook his ugly head dolefully.

"Aye," he growled, "your foolish prattle may
have a word of truth for once, but forget not,
my fat Benjamin, that it rains also, and rain is
wet, aye in sooth, 'tis very wet"—and again he
turned over his coat.

Benjamin tipped his pewter pot to his lips.

"Granted it is wet, Simon, but its wetness bears
out the very wisdom of my forbearance with it."

"How so, prattler?"

" 'Tis simple, Simon. The rain that rains without will never rain within, and being within, we
well can scoff at the rain without, considering
only the good which it doeth to the fields, as
yonder yokel will vouch. I'll lay me he welcomes the rain that will ease his plowing labors."

Simon looked at the yokel.

"Aye, he's welcoming it with its kind, each time he hears it. See how he spits. Methinks your rain without is raining within now, Benjamin," and he chuckled hoarsely.

"Simon Grappletight, your wit astoundeth me," Benjamin said sarcastically. "You ought to drink this Kentish ale more frequent. 'Tis plain it stimulates your brain somewhat. And faith it needs it."

"Gr-r," growled Simon like a dog at bay. He leaned forward to turn his coat once more, then suddenly he sat up straight and stiff.

"H'st! H'st!"

Benjamin's head jerked up. His ears seemed to twitch themselves forward. His eyes turned to the door, all the sparkle gone from them, and his hand tightened on his pistol butt.

Was it fancy, or was that a clatter on the cobbles outside? What made the man sleeping at the window lift his head slightly? Was it possible that, hidden in the shadow, his eyes were not closed, but were watching the two men seated by the fireside?

A guilty conscience sees an enemy in every man. Benjamin leaned towards Simon.

"See that man in the corner," he whispered. "Dost think he truly is asleep?"

Simon looked swiftly across at the reclining figure. A soft, rumbling snore seemed to throb through a second's silence in the storm.

The long man breathed easier.

"Thy nerves are shaken, poor fool," he breathed, with an accompanying curse. "Drink up thy ale, man, 'twill help to steady thee."

Benjamin raised his mug once more, then suddenly lowered it again, as another warning "H'st!" broke from Simon.

Clatter, clatter, went hoofs upon the cobbles outside.

There was no mistaking it this time. Some one was there. Horses were at the door of the "Whyte Hart."

Simon Grappletight looked fixedly at Benjamin Greenleaf. Benjamin Greenleaf looked fixedly at Simon Grappletight. The faces of both men tightened. Gone was the careless mien of a moment before.

" 'Tis he," muttered Greenleaf.

"And another," growled Grappletight.

"And mebee more," sighed Greenleaf.

" 'Twould lose our guineas," groaned Grappletight.

"The devil!" wailed Greenleaf.

Something meant to be a smile contorted the long man's scarred features. He growled when he saw that the fat little fellow was shaking.

"Don't forget the hundred guineas. 'Tis ours for the taking. One pistol shot straight and true is all that is wanted."

The thin lips formed the words, and the little man's shiver of apprehension became less apparent.

"You're sure you'll know him again," whispered Greenleaf.

"Aye," answered Simon. "I'd know him in a thousand."

At that instant, the door thundered beneath mighty blows. Above the uproar rose a man's voice; an impatient, powerful voice.

"Ho! landlord. Ho! man. The door—the door! Unbolt, unbolt, quick man! Zounds, this rain."

With a scurry and a scuffle, Joe Watkins, the landlord, bustled into the taproom and hastened to the door.

"Who be there?" he called, with his red hands on the bolts, and his red nose against the timbers.

"Travelers, dolt," came the reply, "and well nigh drenched by this accursed rain. Open man, quick, and there's good gold awaiting for you."

Joe hastily undid the bolts, and the wayfarers entered.

There were two of them. One was tall and strapping, well made, and handsome of feature. His shoulders were broad, his body big, and his legs long. His face was clean cut—though in truth it bore traces of dissipation—his brow high and his hair black and crisp beneath his three-cornered hat. He wore no wig, but he was obviously an aristocrat. His finely cut and gorgeously broidered riding coat spoke to his high rank, and even were this not sufficient, there was no gainsaying the modishness of his wonderful cravat, or the costliness of his dangling cuffs of lace.

He was undoubtedly a dandy, probably from London or Paris, though withal a sturdy figure of a man. His age would be about thirty.

Behind him came his servant—a stout-built fellow with expressionless face, red side-whiskers and redder nose. His hat was already off, and his hair was also red. He looked a man in the early thirties, and fully as strong as his master.

Benjamin Greenleaf viewed them askance from the corner of his eye.

"In faith, a hefty pair," he murmured, very, very softly.

"Grr-r-r!" growled Simon.

"Bid your hosteler see to our horses," said the dandy, "and bring us some of your Kentish ale—

'tis warming, so they say, and by my snuff-box
we need it. What say you, Peter?"

"I say zookers, 'twill be welcome, my lord.
Aye, zizzers 'twill."

"And likewise zotters 'twill, and also zanders
'twill, Peter, my rascal," echoed his master, hurl-
ing a chair towards the fire and throwing himself
down in it.

He shook the wet from his coat and threw it
to his man, who spread it out before the blaze.

The dandy took a pinch of snuff from a jeweled
box, and dusted his cravat with the fragment of
gorgeous lace that served as a kerchief.

Simon eyed him narrowly.

"An ill night," he growled.

My lord looked up quickly, and ran his gaze
over the two men.

"Aye! friend," he said slowly. "It's an ill
night—but 'twere well if it got no more ill, for
we travel further to-night."

Simon lowered his lids, but Benjamin answered
for him.

"'Twere hard to tell, master. Methinks myself the illest part of an ill night is the early
morn."

The aristocrat laughed loudly.

"In truth you put it queerly, but withal 'tis
demmed true, friend. What say you, Peter?"

"I say zookers, m'lord, and I hope 'twill get no worse."

"And likewise ziggers, Peter! I echo thee!"

The landlord brought their ale, and they drank it in silence, the while Simon smoked and watched.

And none noticed that the yokel had left the inn as the travelers entered, and that the man asleep at the window had shifted his position, as if the better to observe them.

"Dost tarry long here, master?" ventured Simon.

"But time to give the nags a feed and a breath. Then on to Orpington—'tis but ten miles. And you? Are you for London?"

Simon shook his head.

"We're but for Westerham," he said. "And faith, we must away if we're to reach our journey's end ere midnight."

He looked viciously at Benjamin, and the little fat man sighed.

"'Tis true," he groaned. "We must away, and I was but getting comfortable, and settling in a doze before this fire."

Simon stood up.

"You've been in a doze well nigh all your life, porpoise," he growled. "As witness your rolls of fat. I pity more that ass you ride upon to-night than you."

"Belike you have a fellow-feeling for it," quoth Benjamin, sighing again. "And 'tis well you ride a tall nag, for otherwise your own great hoofs would be trailing in the mud."

Simon fumed, but heeding him not, the little man bowed before m'lord.

"I leave to you my portion of the blaze, sir," he said.

Simon donned his hat.

" 'Tis a pity you cannot take it with you, porker. You are forever frizzling your fat before the flames."

A comical expression of pained resignation spread itself over the little man's features.

"So I am. So I am," he admitted, wearily. "But, mark you, Simon, the reason it is plain."

"For why then, dolt?" demanded Simon, twirling his riding crop.

Benjamin edged well away from it.

"Because, simple Simon, I prefer to do my frizzling in this world—while you, alack! alack! waiteth for the next."

M'lord roared his merriment.

" 'Tis good policy, friend, and faith, I think I'll adopt it for myself," and he drew nearer to the fire.

"Aye, 'tis good policy, sir," went on the little man. "But 'tis hard to practice with a man like Simon Grappletight on your heels. Even now he hounds me from this dear warmth into the wet without."

"But you leave the more blaze for me," quoth m'lord. "So everything hath its compensations, friend."

"Aye, aye," murmured Benjamin, "even rain—wet rain—see how 'twill cleanse poor Simon's face. 'Tis strange indeed the contrariness of nature, both human and otherwise. How we hate the wet, and how we love it. Simon hates it, and I love it. Aye, but 'tis in a pewter mug I love it. Hast ever thought that when out we came in to get wet within, and when in we go out to get wet without, and when we are wet within we want not to be wet without, yet still when we are wet without we like also to be wet within? Yet gladly would I be dry within if 'twere but dry without," and he sighed long and deeply, while Simon scowled.

M'lord roared in merriment.

"Thy philosophy hath a practical trend, good friend," he said. "What say you, Peter?"

"I say zookers, m'lord," burst out Peter, dumbfounded by the unexpected flow of eloquence from the little man.

"And likewise ziggers," quoth the philosopher, as he donned his hat. "Adieu, fair sir."

"Farewell," grunted Simon, struggling into his great coat, and stretching his limbs for the last time before the tempting flames.

"Nay! Au revoir!" called the young lord genially. "Mayhap we'll meet again."

Simon stopped at the door and looked back with a queer expression on his face.

"Aye, mayhap we will, master. 'Tis like as not."

And his little companion shivered again, though the door was not yet open to the howling wind.

Then the bolts rattled, the gusts blew across the room, the rain spray splashed the floor, the ill-assorted pair passed out, and the door banged heavily.

After this, the silent, sleepy man by the window seemed to move his head in his doze. It was almost as if he were looking out through the knotted glass vanes.

DESCRIBES A MOST REMARKABLE ENCOUNTER

"A TRULY strange pair o' adventurers, Peter," essayed m'lord after the clatter of hoofs had died away in the distance.

"Aye, sire," answered Peter; "and, faith, I'd rather meet them in this inn than on the lonesome highway."

"That fat fellow was a merry soul," went on his master. "But I did not like the visage of the long knave."

At that moment the landlord's pretty daughter, Betty, entered, bearing a steaming plate of soup for each of the two wayfarers.

She was a sweet-faced maid, with black hair and eyes, and red but timid-looking little lips. She seemed nervous at being thus called upon to serve so high as m'lord, for when he looked up and caught her eye she flushed red, and stumbled so that she nearly spilled the soup.

It was strange, too, that m'lord's cheeks also burned, and he turned away quickly.

After she had served them, however, he beck-

oned her to him, his composure having quite returned.

"I did not know that you had anything to do
with this place," he said. "Is your father the
landlord?"

Betty nodded, and went redder than ever.

"Ah," went on m'lord. "I wondered where
you'd gone when you left my kitchen." He
paused as he saw the tears start to her eyes, and
then went on hurriedly. "But now this place will
have a new attraction."

The girl made as if to speak, but her courage
seemed to fail her and she turned away abruptly.
M'lord was about to say something more, but
he, too, thought better of it, and snapped his
white teeth instead.

The appetizing smell of the soup wafted across
the room and reached the nostrils of the man by
the window.

He raised his head and sniffed the air. Then,
with a yawn, he stood up and stretched his limbs,
looking the while towards the window.

He was a huge fellow. Not so burly, either, as
he was broad and tall. Suddenly, he turned and
faced the firelight, gazing fixedly down at the two
men sitting.

And as he gazed, the young lord lifted his eyes
and looked back at him. For a second he sat

quite still, then slowly he, too, rose to his feet, his
hands leaning on the small table whereon the
landlord's daughter had served the supper.

His eyes were staring now—staring amaze-
struck at the man by the window.

And m'lord's mouth hung agape.

The other was passing his hand wearily-like
across his forehead. He seemed as in a daze.

Slowly, very slowly, m'lord raised a quivering
finger and pointed at him.

"Speak!" he gasped, hoarsely. "Speak, man!
Who are you?"

Again the weary motion of the other's hand
across his brow.

He gave a jerky laugh.

"Egad!" he muttered. "Methinks 'tis hard to
say. But a moment since I thought I was myself, but now 'twould seem instead that I am
you."

Silence for a moment.

"Aye," echoed the young lord, in a low voice;
"and did you but wear my clothes you'd be my
very self indeed."

He turned to his man, who had spilled his ale
in his amaze, and was staring at the two in dull
perplexity.

"And what say you, Peter?"

Peter drew a deep breath.

"I say zookers, m'lord, and likewise ziggers and zotters and zanders, and a dozen others, and, by God! 'twere worthy of them all, and more."

"Aye, Peter; 'tis queer, 'tis mighty queer. Tell me, friend, do I see aright, or am I blinded by my very vainness?"

The stranger laughed again. A rich laugh it was, emitted by a deep and booming voice.

"Methinks, m'lord, we are each other's double," he said. "I've heard that each of us hath one somewhere in this world, but faith, I never thought to meet mine this night."

"Nor I," quoth his lordship. "Sit you down and tell me who you are, and see if we can fathom the wherefores of this strange resemblance. But first you'll sup with us. Nay! I'll have no refusal. Such a meeting cannot be ended without a-breaking bread."

The stranger turned his face to hide the eager look of hunger in his eyes.

He seated himself.

"Who I am, m'lord, matters but little. Folks I once called friends knew me as John Shale, of Dene Farm. But that is some time since. To-night I am John Shale of the Whyte Hart, to-morrow I may be John Shale of Sevenoaks, or Orpington, or Westerham, or Chistlehurst, or whereso'er my fancy pleaseth."

"And why hast given up farming, friend Shale?", asked his lordship.

" 'Twas not of my doing, m'lord. The lease was up. The farm was in the best condition. My debts, left me by my father, were well nigh all repaid, and so my landlord took it to himself. 'Tis the law," he added, bitterly.

The other frowned.

" 'Twas a scurvy trick," he vowed. "And, prithee, who was your landlord?"

A hard look came into John Shale's eyes.

"His name is Clayville—Sir Humphrey Clayville," he said, in a low voice. "Perchance you've heard of him. His manor is at Orpington."

The young lord looked up in surprise.

"Why! Clayville. He soon will be a kinsman of mine," he cried. "I am betrothed to his niece. Within a few days I hope to make her my bride."

John Shale sat up.

"Ah, then you must be Lord Anderley, of Bessels Green," he ejaculated.

The other bowed.

"Lord Geoffrey Anderley," he replied, "at your service."

"You are a lucky man," quoth Shale. "They say the Lady Gloria Clayville is very beautiful. 'Twere even known down here to us, in rustic Kent, that her loveliness hath taken London by storm. 'Tis said even the king is enamored of her."

Anderley laughed.

"Faith, so 'tis said, man; but, an' you believe it or not, I myself cannot vouch either way."

"What meanest thou?" ejaculated the farmer in amazement. "Is she not soon to be your wife?"

"Aye, right soon, I hope, but ne'ertheless the pleasure of seeing her for the first time hath yet to be mine. To this day I have not seen her face, nor she seen mine."

Shale sat back in perplexity.

"Well, 'tis strange," he said, "but that is thy affair, m'lord."

M'lord laughed a trifle loudly.

"Nay, 'tis not of my making, anyway, friend. For nigh three months now I've striven to see the lady, but ever the little minx hath arranged it that we should not meet."

"And yet you are going to marry her soon?"

"So 'tis said, friend; and, in sooth, I am keenly anxious for the time to come, so much have I heard of her beauty. Folks say she is comely of form as well as sweet of face, and that she rides a horse better than any man in the hunt. 'Tis said also she shoots straight as a die, and rumor hath it that in a bantering mood she fought a sword bout with an aged

gallant, an' her own hand in wedlock was to be
his reward should be outmatch her. But, faith,
she trounced him soundly."

And M'lord Anderley laughed loud and long.

A deep frown furrowed itself across John
Shale's face. His curiosity was whetted by the
other's strange story, but he felt something like
repugnance for the distorted mind which could
repeat distasteful gossip about the woman it
ought by every law of mankind to revere. Even
though m'lord had never seen his future wife,
and was yet betrothed to her, it was not to his
credit that he should discuss her qualities,
whether good or bad, with one who was an absolute stranger, and at that far beneath himself in station—though not (so trusted Shale)
in sense of honor of womenfolk.

Still it was queer that his lordship should have
contemplated marriage with a woman he had
never seen, however much repute might sing her
praises.

Anderley now called loudly for the landlord,
and when he appeared commanded him to bring
a flagon of burgundy, which he insisted upon
sharing with the young farmer.

" 'Tis a night for wine," the dandified aristocrat said, as he filled up two bumpers. "And,

moreover, I would have you drink with me the health of my lady."

He stood up and raised his glass.

"To her who is willing to wed any man who can beat her at swordplay."

Shale flushed.

"Nay, m'lord," he ventured, "consider it's your future wife you pledge."

Anderley looked at him with elevated brows.

"Aye," he said, slowly, "go on."

The farmer sat back in his chair and toyed with the fragile stem of his glass.

" 'Tis plain, m'lord," he said, his deep voice low but distinct, "you know not who I am. This is a place unseemly for the mention of your lady's name. 'Twere more in keeping, p'raps, if you but permitted me to drink to your future happiness."

Anderley looked at him long and steadily.

John Shale returned the stare with equal steadiness.

"Wouldst try to teach me manners?" said m'lord slowly and ominously.

His man, Peter, rose to his feet and stood back.

Shale looked at him.

"Keep thy seat, man," he said, in calm voice. "There is nought to excite thyself over." He turned to Anderley. "Methinks you know your manners well enough, m'lord. 'Tis a matter of small account to me. 'Twere for you to resent the sporting of thy lady's name in places such as this tavern. For myself I would but refrain from giving thee offense by making her the subject of a common toast."

Again that long, steady look—that ominous silence. The tension was nerve-trying, but the farmer toyed with his glass as before, while Anderley's fingers itched around the jeweled hilt of his sword.

At last m'lord spoke.

"I have it in my mind to teach thee a lesson," he said.

Shale looked at him, then shrugged his shoulders.

"That were a simple matter, m'lord, but 'twere not half so simple as drinking to thine own happiness. Come! raise your glass."

Anderley gave a gesture of impatience.

"Dost know I am accounted one of the finest blades in England?"

The farmer bowed.

" 'Tis a great honor, m'lord."

"And yet," went on the maddened man, " 'tis not so great as to prevent me mixing steel with such as you."

"The victory would be too easy for thee, m'lord."

"Dost scoff at me, knave?"

"Nay, rather am I filled with dire foreboding."

"You carry a sword, man. Is it but for show?"

"Partly, m'lord, the which to impress mine enemies and avoid useless bloodshed; partly to insure their swift despatch."

"Ah, then you know how to use it?"

Shale smiled.

" 'Twere useless to carry steel an' I cannot play it."

"Then show me how to wield it, knave."

Now Shale laughed, and shook his head.

"Nay, m'lord, you need no showing. You know full well. Are you not one of England's greatest swordsmen?"

Anderley flushed.

"Draw man, draw!" he called in rage. "Enough of this senseless parley. You'd teach me manners a moment a-gone. Well, now 'tis I will do the teaching."

Shale's face turned a trifle grim.

"Nay, m'lord, I have no quarrel with thee. Besides, I would far rather refrain from fighting with a man upon his wedding eve."

M'lord was purple now, and tugged furiously at his sword.

"Out man, out! It matters not to me what happens on the morrow, since I'll transfix thee in a trice to-night. Quick, fool, on guard!"

Out flashed his blade, and quivered in the candle-light.

Now, seeing that further argument was useless, Shale slowly withdrew his own rapier and stepped back a pace.

"M'lord, I salute you," he said, bowing low in approved dueling fashion.

There was a click—the ring of steer upon steel—the quick shuffling of riding boots upon the oaken floor—the clink, clink of spurs—keen eyes—tense faces—firm wrists—rasping foils—and the two men were at bay.

And the face of one before the fight was as the face of the other. But now m'lord's visage was contorted with rage beyond all recognition. A diabolical gleam was in his eyes—his brows knitted fiercely—his breath, quick, eager pants. His left hand twitched and clenched and started open again. He was a man on murder bent.

But the farmer—he fought with a smile upon his lips (though withal it was a grim one), his head high, his hat—the tall, furry and unkempt hat—held lightly and gracefully in his left hand.

'Twas as if he played with buttoned foils, in gentle practice bout.

Now m'lord presses the attack, thrusting viciously and cunningly, playing for an opening and darting eagerly into it, but always to be outmatched in the nick of time. Now he is on guard, fighting fiercely and skillfully against the bewildering swiftness of the other man's attack.

Then once more the farmer fencer falls back, and his smile seems broader. Seeing this, Anderley becomes so maddened he well nigh neglects his skill, and beats heavily, brutally, and almost irresistibly, against the whirling steel which, shimmering in the candle-light, seems as a great circular shield in front of John Shale's face.

But through that barrier of steel these eyes now twinkle merrily, and, observing this, grim despair falls upon the face of Anderley, for full well he knows that the merriment in these eyes bespeaks the confidence of this ill-bred farmer to lay low "one of England's greatest blades."

Peter, standing stolidly by the door, ready to prevent the landlord from intervening, should he feel so disposed, realized, almost as soon as m'lord himself, that his master was a beaten man.

As he looked at the wonderful exhibition of sword play given by the farmer, he found himself inspired with unwilling admiration, and 'twas with greatest difficulty that he prevented himself on more than one occasion from crying out in approval at some particularly brilliant piece of fencing.

Shale was still defending himself easily and confidently, turning aside the frantic attacks of m'lord with as little concern as he would divert the untutored thrusts of a hot-headed schoolboy.

Suddenly, the landlord thrust open the door from the back rooms and rushed in, full of excitement. When he realized what was taking place, he lifted up his hands with a wail of apprehension.

"In God's name cease, gentlemen!" he cried. "Consider what I am to do with one of you dead upon my hands."

He danced around the fighters in a paroxysm of distress.

"Stand back, host," called Shale, "else 'tis you who will be dead upon our hands." But the frantic man paid no attention to him.

Then Peter thrust his long, strong arm out and seized him by the scruff of the neck.

"Zookers, man, would'st have thyself transfixed upon a yard of steel?" he shouted, thrusting him back against the wall.

Joe struggled in vain, and there he was held firmly while he wrung his fat hands in despair, cursing John Shale with every oath he considered could safely be used in the presence of quality. Being held in check by m'lord's retainer, he deemed it wise to make it plain that 'twas on the farmer he did rain his curses.

The sweat was standing out on Anderley's brow now—but it was cold sweat. He fought as he had never fought before, pressing attack upon attack, feint upon feint, and thrust upon thrust, but never once did he penetrate that steel barrier or turn aside the purpose of that sure blade.

And the farmer was as cool as ever—as imperturbed as when he lay asleep and unnoticed upon the wooden window seat.

Suddenly, m'lord thought he saw an opening. It was a wonderful chance, for Shale's sword for a second was down and his body unguarded.

Like a flash the keen-pointed rapier leapt straight at the farmer's heart, driven with all the viciousness of a strong man's strength behind it.

Peter gave a hoarse cry.

The landlord shut his eyes with a quick gasp of horror.

Next instant m'lord had stumbled forward irresistibly. Like a streak of lightning Shale's wrist had risen. His blade had flashed, and the other's rapier had passed harmlessly under his left arm.

Anderley, overcome by the force of his own thrust, fell forward a step, and in that instant he felt his weapon seized in a firm grasp, and the pointed steel of the farmer's sword glittered within an inch of his white throat.

And so they stood for a full ten seconds.

At last m'lord raised his head high with proud mien.

"Strike!" he gasped. "Strike hard and true."

But, still with that soft smile upon his lips, Shale lowered his sword and slowly and silently replaced it in its scabbard.

M'lord stared at him in bewilderment.

The farmer turned to the table whereon the glasses of wine still stood, and, grasping that which had been his, he raised it aloft.

"M'lord, I drink to thee and to thy future happiness. Methinks I have the right now."

Wearily, Anderley dashed the sweat from his brow, and then bowed gracefully in acknowledgment of the toast.

This done, he crossed to the table, and in his turn raised his glass. 'Twas harder to admit defeat like this than face an honest death.

"To the greatest swordsman in England," he said, in a low voice.

And this time 'twas Farmer Shale who bowed gracefully—quite as gracefully as m'lord had done.

IN WHICH A MAID SHEDS TEARS

JOE WATKINS was scurrying around, arranging the table, carrying in a huge joint of beef and steaming potatoes. He was so happy at the pleasant turn affairs had taken that he did not really know what to be doing.

"It sure be fine to see you a-sittin' quietly at your supper, m'lord," he ventured, as Anderley resumed his meal.

"It sure be, host," repeated Anderley. "For the which both you and I must thank our friend here."

Suddenly, he stood up again and looked at Shale.

"Why your hat on, friend—and your coat fastened up?"

Shale smiled grimly.

"Ah, well, m'lord, 'tis time I got upon my way."

Anderley flushed.

"Nay, man, nay! I pray thee be seated. Hast not been enough upon your feet this night. And hark, the wind blows fiercer than ever. And

30

see also, mine host hath shown himself an excellent cook. 'Tis nigh an insult to leave such serving undevoured."

Shale bowed.

"Truly, you have an honest heart, m'lord."

"Heart be demmed, 'tis little reward for saving my life to ask you to sup with me."

"Saving your life, m'lord," laughed Shale. "In truth, 'tis a pleasant way to put it."

"But withal a true one!" added m'lord. "For he who spares a life leaves to live a life and thus doth save a life for living, e'en though that life were worthy but of death."

Shale seated himself at the table.

"Pardieu, m'lord, but you have a quaint way of phrasing it. Reminds me somewhat of yon well-fed rascal who with his murderous-looking companion consumed a gallon of ale while perched on this same seat."

"He was indeed a merry rogue," quoth Anderley, "but stagger me, man, was that 'Pardieu' you said? Faith, our farmer breathes French oaths like a native, Peter. Hark at him an' please God that it may cure thee of thy everlasting 'zookers.' What say you, man?"

Peter fumbled with his spoon, then at last blurted out.

"I say zookers, please you, m'lord."

Anderley slapped his thigh so hard that his mirth ended abruptly in a pretty oath.

"Egad, Peter, you are veritably hopeless."

He turned to Shale suddenly.

"Hast been to court," he demanded.

The farmer flushed.

"That were impossible, m'lord."

"Then how came you by the French oath, and with the true Paris intonation too? 'Tis common enough in London, but I did not look to find it here amidst the wheat fields, and the hop fields— bless 'em—of Kent. Nay, do not think to mislead me, man, I mean to know."

Shale laughed.

" 'Twas one I heard my father use most frequent."

"Your father, faith, and how did he acquire the knack o't? This grows interesting."

The farmer looked far away into the blazing fire.

"He learned it at the French court, m'lord. There he also learned to fence, and in time taught me. He had such a knack of it that he was commissioned to the court for the purpose of instructing young gallants there—why, what's amiss, m'lord?"

Anderley was staring at him strangely. His

eyes told of some strong emotion stirring him as he gazed at the young farmer.

At last he looked away.

"What's amiss! 'Tis nothing but a passing notion, that is all—a strange idea, an unexpected brilliance of my brain."

He gulped down a spoonful of hot potatoes, thereby burning his throat so badly that he gasped for breath fully half a minute while his lips formed unspoken curses.

Peter sprang to his assistance and came in for a severe punch in the ribs from m'lord which brought an anguished "zookers" to his lips.

Shale went on eating.

" 'Tis plain 'tis my words that have affected you so strangely, m'lord," he said, "though why I cannot say. But if it is aught that may concern me prithee why not unfold it to my ears."

But Anderley had recovered his composure by now and waved his hand airily.

" 'Tis nought of importance, my friend. Mayhap 'twill never cause me to comment upon it. But again perchance I may tell thee of my thoughts some day, who knows?"

"Who knows, m'lord," repeated Shale, resolving not to press the matter, though he knew it must have held some strange import.

They went on eating in silence for a little

time, then, the meal completed, Anderley sat back with a sigh.

"Well, friend, 'tis nigh the end of a very pleasant meeting and one that will linger long in my memory. The storm seems to have abated somewhat—though, gadzooks, 'tis black enough yet without—and 'tis nigh time faithful Peter and myself were on our way."

"And I, too, m'lord," responded Shale. "But ere you go let me bid you ride with your hand on your holster, and a keen eye on the road."

Anderley looked at him curiously.

"'Tis sound advice, but what inspires it, friend?"

Shale sat back also.

"Remember you when you spoke for a short space with yon ill-matched pair of rascals."

"Well, what o' it?"

"Just this, m'lord, at that time I seemed to slumber on the window seat, but, faith, my eyes were well agape and my ears were listening hard."

"Go on."

"And what I heard, though 'twas but little and may have meant less, made me suspicious that the twain were not above enriching themselves by means other than honest, m'lord."

"At my expense, mean you?"

" 'Twere possible, for when you entered they evinced no little interest in you, and displayed no little concern that so sound a man as your faithful server accompanied you."

M'lord stroked his chin thoughtfully.

"Ah, well," he said at last. "If we're not fit to account for two such dogs as these, i' faith we're better dead—eh, Peter?"

Peter started.

"Eh, m'lord!" he ejaculated, "no, m'lord—I mean—zookers, yes, m'lord."

Anderley rose to his feet and donned his great riding coat. This done he held out his hand and wrung Shale's in a warm grasp.

"Once more my thanks, friend, for this my life," he said, "though demme if I know why you spared it. 'Twere worthless enough."

"Perhaps 'twere but remarkable cunning on my part, m'lord," smiled Shale, "for with you a corpse I'd have but ghosts to haunt me for my supper, whereas with you alive I am indeed another man, as well fed as thy fav'rite dog."

Anderley laughed, and laughing tossed a guinea to mine host and moved towards the door.

Joe Watkins scurried before him to see that the horses were awaiting and when he had passed out into the now drizzling rain, but still black

night, m'lord paused to say a last farewell to
Shale.

At that instant pretty Betty Watkins ran into
the taproom and crossed swiftly to the door.

"M'lord," she murmured, "Good m'lord.
Could I have converse with thee but a moment."

The self-satisfied look faded from Anderley's
face and was replaced by a frown of impatience.

"Another time, sweet miss, another time," he
drawled. "Aye, come and see me at the hall.
If 'tis to enter my service again you desire, why
Peter here will speak with you."

Tears—tears of mortification and sorrow
started quickly to poor Betty's eyes as she turned
away.

"Nay, m'lord," she murmured, "'tis you and
only you will do."

But now Anderley had waved good night to
Shale, and was already braving the storm.

Peter looked once at Betty with sorrowful
eyes like a faithful dog, then followed his master
silently.

As Anderley seized his horse's bridle and
swung into the saddle a black frown overspread
his handsome features.

"Peter," he growled, "an' one day, perchance
you should grow rich and still would have an

easy mind, take heed what I say, man, and beware all women."

Peter's horse clattered out into the roadway.
Perhaps it was well for him his master could not
see his face.

"Aye, zookers, m'lord," he said, "though in
truth some o' these women be but poor helpless
creatures.   And she is a winsome little maid,
m'lord."

Lord Anderley cut viciously at his horse.

"You're a fool, man," he grunted.

"Zookers, that I be, m'lord," whispered Peter,
then softly—"Poor Betty."

His two cheeks were wet, but it was not the
rain that made them so—Poor Peter.

DEALS WITH A DIRTY NIGHT AND A
DESPERATE FIGHT

AS the door crashed heavily behind Lord Anderley and his man, Joe Watkins turned and looked queerly at his daughter.

"What I'd like to know is what them tears are in your eyes for," he said sharply.

Betty swung round abruptly and dashing her hand to the offending drops trickling down her cheeks, she ran from the room.

Her father looked after her for a long time and, watching him, John Shale saw his face gradually go pale and his hands clench swiftly.

Suddenly he turned to the farmer.

"There's summat amiss with my girl," he said, "an' I can't just get the hang of it."

Shale answered with a lightness he was far from feeling.

"For sooth, 'tis a common complaint love-sickness. My lord's man seemed a fine set-up fellow with kindly manners. 'Tis small wonder the girl is smitten."

Joe Watkins was far from reassured.

38

" 'Tis queer like, she's been like that ever since she was a kitchen maid at Anderley Hall. And I don't just know why she left there either. There's summat wrong that's what there is. Strikes me you're right, and that big fellow, Peter, has summat to do with it. Well, if he's been foolin' wi' my Betty there's agoin' to be trouble 'twixt me an' him." And Joe brought his mighty fist down on his counter with a resounding smack that rattled the glasses in the bar so loud that poor Betty in her little attic bedroom above heard the noise and, fearing the questioning of her stern father, turned white and wondered how long it would be before he learned her secret and turned her from his house.

Shale had no wish to let Watkins guess his own suspicions and, as the landlord set about stamping out the fire and snuffing the candles, he decided that he could not reasonably remain within the shelter of the inn any longer. Accordingly, he fastened up his coat collar and prepared to depart.

Watkins opened the door for him and bade him a curt "Good night." He really viewed the departure of the stranger with something like relief, for it seemed to the honest soul that misfortune had dogged his footsteps during the whole time this tall fellow, who bore such a strange resemblance to the Lord Anderley, had been in the inn.

He watched the farmer stride across the cobbled yard and fade into the darkness, then once more the great door clashed, and there was only the ceaseless drizzle of the rain and the fitful whistling of the wind.

The night was in very truth a black one.

"Black as the devil," quoth Shale as he marched sturdily along the highway. "An' I'll warrant me Cloven-hoof himself is not afar off either."

He shivered and stretched out his hands to feel if he was still walking by the hedgerow.

"Oft have I been abroad at midnight," he mused, "but never have I felt the chill in my bones as on this accursed night. I have the feeling there shall be dire happenings ere 'tis o'er, aye, even more dire than those which have already taken place, and, faith, they were bad enow."

He stumbled into a deep pool of rain under the overhanging branches of a mighty oak tree and swore deep and long. He was at a stretch in the lonely road where woods bordered either side of the last dip in the road before the gentle rise into the quaint village of ancient Sevenoaks.

He tried to shake off the eeriness which possessed him by pondering upon the happenings at the inn, but he could not rid himself of the queer feeling, the presentiment of ill to come. He had to strain his eyes so that he should not stumble into the tall, thick, overshadowing hedge, that 'twas well nigh impossible for him to center his thoughts on anything else. He looked up overhead to see if there was any rift in the blackness of the night, but there was none and he stumbled on as before.

The rain fell in a dreary drizzle, the sound of which was magnified a thousand-fold by its alighting on the leafy bed of the dark, gloomy woods. Every now and again the soft mournful sighing of the wind could be heard afar off, gradually strengthening to a fierce, gruesome wail as it rushed through the branches of the trees, and passed on shrieking and moaning into the drear deadness of the night. And the rain drizzled on, and the way seemed blacker than ever and the gaunt trees more silent—like great, gloomy sentinels in the pitchness.

What was that?

A deep rumbling far in the distance.

The weary wind wailed and shrilled again and the grim trees shook their shadowy arms ominously.

Again that queer, queer rumbling noise like a dread drone afar, afar.

Shale stopped and stood stock still. And the silence seemed but the more chillsome now that the plash—plash—plash of his feet in the murky pools had ceased.

But still that strange rumbling throbbed through the black night air. It rose and it fell with deadly monotony, and always it was agrowing the louder.

Suddenly Shale laughed, but jerkily. Then he listened again and laughed once more in quick relief.

And now he roared his laughter loud out into the night.

"John, my lad, methinks you are a greater coward than you thought. 'Tis nought but a coach or chaise, and your very hair stood up as though it were taking old Horny-pow himself for a ride at midnight."

He carefully felt his way to the side of the road, and stood close into the hedge to let the vehicle pass.

And now he could hear it rumbling and rattling a-down the highway, not a hundred yards off.

Of an instant there was a brilliant flash of red flame through the densy blackness, and then the brutal bark of a pistol. A horse snorted and shrieked—there was the grinding of sliding wheels on the road, the hoarse shouts of postillions, and a garble of yells and cries.

Shale stood motionless for a second, then he started to run swiftly towards the scene of the tumult—heedless of the darkness and splashing the rainwater from the pools as he went.

The noise came nearer and nearer.

He was about fifty yards from the spot—though in truth he could see nothing before him but the pitchy blackness, when suddenly a slim, slight figure loomed up immediately in front of him, and in the fraction of a second, crashed into his arms.

For a moment he was dazed by the impact, and he found himself with his arms clasped firmly about a soft yielding body. He held it tightly out of fear that it would slip to the ground, and strangely there was a rift in the black clouds above and a shimmering light slid through. The dawn was at hand. Now he looked down and he realized that a head was pressed against his breast. He could see and feel that it was curly, and the soft first morning gleam lighting upon it was reflected and told him it was yellow— yellow like gold.

As he looked, she raised her face to his. It was

a girlish face, and its beauty made John Shale draw his breath quickly. The eyes were large, round eyes, brown or black or violet, he wasn't sure which, and they were open wide as if in terror. They searched his face and seared into his very soul, and the lovely red lips quivered the while.

And as they saw his countenance, his honest blue eyes, his shock of black crisp hair, his reassuring gaze, his simple homespun scarf, and his quaint dilapidated tall, furry hat, the fear faded from her face.

She pushed herself back from him.

"Tell me," she whispered hurriedly—"you—you are not one of them?"

He shook his head.

"Nay, my lady, I am but a lone wayfarer who chanced to hear pistols and oaths, and hied himself hither lest there should be some little need for his strong right arm. And methinks there is."

There were louder shouts through the darkness, shouts of men approaching, hearing which the girl shuddered.

"Listen," she gasped, "an' you would save me from ill, help me to escape yonder rabble. I have fled me from them posthaste, but they have followed me from Bessels Green and, riding hard, o'ertook my chaise and halted it by shooting one of the leaders. In the confusion and darkness I escaped, but they are searching for me now. Wilt aid me?"

He bowed low with courtly grace, and a look of quick relief lit up her face.

"Quick," she cried, "we must fly. They are close upon us."

He seized her hand, and together they ran rapidly along the road.

But their pursuers had heard their footsteps now, and with hoarse cries dashed after them.

In vain Shale looked as he ran for a break in the thick hedge. They reached the end of the wooded part of the road, and passed from the protecting shadows of the trees into the open, while the morning lights came and went in the skies, and the rain drizzled into nothingness at last.

Mingled with the patter, patter of human feet was now the clatter of horses' hoofs. Their pursuers were mounted.

It was plain that further flight was useless.

"We waste our wind," gasped Shale, "let us halt here where the hedge is thinner, and I will keep the hounds at bay while you strive to beat your way through the bush into the fields beyond."

They stopped by the roadside and next instant their pursuers were upon them.

Shale thrust the girl behind him and drew his rapier.

There were seven mounted men. They leapt from their horses at the command of their leader and, advancing, peered through the gloom.

"Here's the maid, lads, but who's that with her. 'Tis none of our number by his garb. Stand by, stranger, or you'll come by harm."

" 'Tis a remark I might well retort, gentle and honored sir," answered Shale grimly, tucking up the sleeve of his sword arm as he spoke.

The man pushed forward, but stopped as the silver rapier steel flashed out.

"Oddsbooth! would'st defy me, churl," he shouted wrathfully. "Well, a bullet will bring thee to thy senses and take thy senses from thee at one fell blow and, mark me, I have that bullet handy."

He thrust up a long pistol, and his companions laughed loudly at his coarse wit. But now above their laughter rose a girlish voice.

"Dare to shoot, Ned Marley, and I'll have you whipped to-morrow like a dog."

The man wavered and lowered his pistol.

"We have our orders, m'lady," he answered gruffly, "an' they are to bring you back safe and sound. We had no word about this sorry knave."

She was quick to take advantage of his hesitation.

"Then if you would not harm me, shoot not, for should your bullets miss this man 'twere well nigh certain they would find their mark in me. And then, Marley, you would all most surely be whipped and end your miserable lives dangling from a rope, fit objects for the hounds to snap at."

Marley muttered grim oaths, but nevertheless withdrew to the other side of the road, and held a muttered consultation with his men.

"Now's your chance," whispered Shale to the girl, "force your way through the hedge and run along behind it till you come to an inn which is near by, and there you will get shelter."

"While you remain here to be shot?"

He smiled grimly down at her.

"A few will fall 'ere then," he vowed.

She shook her head.

"Nay, friend, I think yours is too good a life to sacrifice. You have proved yourself a friend of mine, and never shall it be said that I deserted my friends. While I am with you, they will not dare to shoot."

The men gathered round them in a semicircle,

the leader, Marley, slightly in advance, though well back from the glittering rapier.

" 'Twill fare ill with you, fellow, if you do not be off," he called, "unless you begone within a minute we'll set about you, and we'll wipe you out. Won't we, lads?"

"Aye," growled the others ominously, "that we will."

"Proceed then," replied Shale, calmly. "I am waiting the first of you with eagerness. Methinks it will be you, friend Marley. Hast said thy prayers? If not, make haste, and look you, 'twould be a charity to some poor churl who perchance might find thee skewered in the road, were you first to discard your handsome broidered coat, which, being yellow, an' I see aright, will be most sadly soiled when thy blood is let out upon it."

Shale heard a little thrill of laughter beside him, and Marley muttered curses under his breath. But withal he stepped back a pace.

"You are over venturesome, Marley," went on Shale tauntingly, "but yet you have a worthy respect for your yellow coat, or is it for my blade—ah, no, I think not, 'tis plain 'tis your own skin you treasure, e'en though it be a very dirty skin, Ned, nigh as dirty as your black heart, which would have you lay your plebeian hands upon a lady."

The taunted man danced about in rage.

"At him, fellows," he shouted, "would'st let one worthless rogue defy the lot o'ye. At him —I say—at him and in a moment you'll o'er-power him."

The others hesitated. 'Twas plain that the first to make the assault would feel the point of that glittering blade within his flesh and none was eager for the honor.

"You go first then, Ned," said one of the rascals, "and we'll follow you."

"Cowards," cried Ned, "six of you, and not one with the courage of a mouse."

"Nay, not six," put in Shale, waggling his sword tantalizingly. "There's seven, Ned. You surely forget yourself, the least venturesome of all. Come be the first, man. I itch to test the temper of my steel upon your rancid flesh."

Marley squirmed like a snake beneath the lash of that taunting tongue, and for a moment it seemed that he would take his little courage in his hands and lead the attack, but even taunts were not enough to bring this about. Instead he drew his pistols and turning presented them at the bodies of his men.

"Get forward, dogs, or I'll drop you where you stand."

There was no gainsaying that the man meant every word he said.

"I'faith, we have an ally, m'lady," quoth John. "Bravo, Ned. But you make an error, man. Shoot them first and order them afterwards, 'twere more in our favor then."

The silvery laughter of m'lady broke the air, and awoke the dormant courage of the men.

"Hark at her scoffing ye," shouted Marley, quick to take advantage—"come on, lads, let's rush him all together, and he can do but little harm."

"Harm!" cried Shale, "in truth he'd do none at all. 'Twould be a charity to rid the earth of the lot of you."

This was too much even for such a chicken-hearted crew, and with hoarse shouts and much brandishing of cudgels they rushed in a mass at the girl's protector.

The latter raised his blade to strike. His face was grim. Only a second more, and——

"Don't kill them, please," sounded softly in his ear.

He looked at her and faltered.

'Twas fatal, for next instant they were under his guard and upon him.

With a soft curse he dropped his sword and struck out fiercely with his naked fists.

The first terrible blow caught Ned Marley full on the jaw and, lifting him well off his feet, drove him stunned back through the ranks of his companions.

The second mighty swipe crashed brutally on the ear of a great clumsy postillion, who had risen on tip-toe to strike with his club. It knocked him sideways against the others, causing the whole crowd to stagger.

One man clutched at Shale's throat.

The latter's mighty hand seized the rogue by the hair of the head and with a splitting shriek he was hurled headlong into the mud.

But now the others were close upon the farmer, around him, behind him. He felt one cunning rascal hurl himself upon his back, but even then he wrestled desperately with two others in front of him.

Backwards and forwards the trio swayed, and with each passing second Shale's long arms, which had wound themselves around the two men before him, were crushing the very life from their bodies.

Down, down he forced them, bending their backs inwards to him till they collapsed suddenly under him, and with a mighty crash he fell on top of them, while the third man still clung upon his back.

At that instant a quivering cry arose in a girlish voice. It ended in a sad, sorrowful wail of despair.

Shale gave a mighty wrench and freed himself from the clutches of the men beneath him. Then his strong right arm struck twice in quick succession heavy brutal blows, and their heads fell back limply.

With the last wretched creature still clinging upon his back like a veritable old man of the sea, Shale staggered drunkenly to his feet. Suddenly, with herculean effort he hurled himself backward on to the muddy ground.

There was a sickening thud, a gasping cry, a soft moaning sound, and the grip of the last man relaxed.

Shale tore himself free and slowly scrambled up.

Four figures lay on the road around him, two silent, two moaning softly.

No one else was to be seen.

With a fierce cry he set off down the road leading through the woods again, but even as he ran he knew he was too late.

While yet a hundred yards off, he heard the shouts of postillions to horses, the clatter of hoofs, the grinding of wheels, and in a few seconds the steady rumbling of a swift-moving chaise.

And Shale knew that it carried away from him a girl with soft eyes and curls of yellow gold.

TELLS OF A STRANGE SCENE IN A WOOD

WITH a hoarse shout, Shale started to run fiercely after the chaise, but the horses were at a gallop and he himself was badly out of breath. After running a hundred yards or so he realized the uselessness of his effort and slowed down.

Who was she, and where had she gone? These were the questions he kept asking himself. She had said the men had followed her from Bessels Green. If such were the case it was well nigh certain they would carry her back to Bessels Green.

His quick wit recollected that Anderley Hall, the seat of Lord Anderley, was at Bessels Green, and there was no other mansion there.

Had the girl come from Anderley Hall? If so, who was she? Was it possible that she could be the Lady Gloria Clayville who was betrothed to Lord Anderley! He couldn't quite tell why the thought haunted him. 'Twas certain that the chaise must have passed Lord Anderley and his servant on its way, but Shale remembered that the former had never seen his bride-to-be, and besides in the darkness of the night he would never dream of stopping a carriage simply to learn who was within it.

Suddenly, it occurred to Shale that he might induce one of the men he had left lying on the road to part with the secret, and he turned back. Besides, he was anxious to make sure that he had not killed any of them.

The dull dawn had broken by the time he reached the scene of his desperate encounter, and when still thirty or forty yards off he saw through the dim light four figures gathered together in the center of the road.

They caught sight of him almost at the same time and, recognizing his tall, furry hat, they greeted him with a volley of oaths.

"Stand back," shouted one, drawing a pistol. "We've had enough of thee and thy meddling this night. If you approach a yard nearer we will riddle you with bullets."

"Aye, that we will," echoed his companions, hastily priming their pistols.

Shale decided it would be advisable to remain where he was and hold parley with them. He had no wish to have a repetition of the scene of a few minutes before, and besides it was a hundred to one that the rogues, in their wrath against him, and with their heads and bones still aching from the blows he had bestowed upon them, would keep their word and shoot him in his tracks.

"An' you believe me, gentlemen," he called, "I was but anxious for your welfare, and returned hither to inquire if you were still alive."

A chorus of growls received his words.

"Aye, we're still alive, though no thanks to you, knave," shouted one of them.

"'Tis a pleasure to hear you say so," answered Shale, "and, prithee, why were you pursuing m'lady in yon impudent fashion?"

"None of your affair," came the response, "an' you'd be wise not to inquire further. Belike by this time she is well on her way back to Anderley Hall. And what dost think M'lady Clayville is to such as you, to boot?"

Shale heard the others turn upon the speaker wrathfully.

"Fool—Dolt—Idiot," they cried. "You've told him who she is."

The man in the tall, furry hat laughed loud enough for them to hear.

"Aye, fool, dolt, idiot, you've told him true, for which he thanks you kindly, and may your hurts be a warning to you ne'er to tackle me again, if so we should chance to meet."

And thus having assured himself that his suspicions were correct and that the girl whom he had held in his arms for that brief second was really and truly the Lady Gloria Clayville, John Shale set out through the wooded road for the third time that morning.

Now the rain had gone, and the wind had ceased to storm, and already the birds were beginning to chirrup in the trees, and the red dawn peeped through the skies and chased away the gloom.

Thus 'twas approaching five o'clock when Shale trudged manfully through the quaint old-world town of Sevenoaks, along its narrow winding streets, and under its overhanging balconies.

He passed through the deserted market square at the top of Tubs Hill and, making his way down the steep decline, he hastened on towards Riverhead.

The previous night he had no fixed idea as to where he was going, though before his vision mighty London had loomed, but now he knew that he was bound for Bessels Green.

'Tis at Riverhead, two miles from Sevenoaks, that the road leading to Bessels Green branches off to the left from the highway. A quarter of a mile from the silent village, the road descends a gentle slope bordered on one side by a deep wood, and on the other by a steep embankment dotted with trees.

It was down this slope that Shale was trudging when suddenly he was startled by the sound of a low moan.

He stopped and stood listening.

No—he was not mistaken—there it was again. The deep groan of a human being in agony.

"Egad. Here's another adventure awaiting my attention," muttered Shale. "They are never ending in number. 'Twould seem there is some one lying in need of succor within these woods."

Again the agonizing sound. Yes, it undoubtedly came from the woods on the left of the road. There was no fence bordering the way and, unimpeded, Shale passed into the dense underbrush and through the trees.

After he had gone about ten yards, he paused and listened. Within a few seconds he heard the moan again, and this time it was close at hand.

Quickly he thrust his way through the bramble bushes and ferns, and passed into a tiny glade with the green grass growing over it.

A strange sight met his gaze—a sight that

filled him with horror, and brought a startled cry from his lips.

In the center of the glade stood a horse grazing lazily, and lying on the ground amidst its feet was the figure of a man, a man sore wounded and bleeding from head and mouth. One twisted foot was held high in the air by the stirrup in which it was caught, and it was plain that the horse had dragged the man along the ground by it.

Shale ran forward and bent on his knees, and looked into the fellow's face. Then, suddenly, he recoiled with a cry of horror.

"My God," he gasped, covering his face with his hands, " 'tis m'lord, M'lord Anderley."

Again he bent and looked down at the poor mutilated features that had once been handsome as his own—their very image—but which were now battered and bruised and bleeding almost beyond recognition.

Now, as he looked the swollen eyes opened and gazed up at him.

"M'lord," Shale said in trembling voice, "what has happened? Can'st speak? How came you by these awful wounds?"

Anderley's blue lips moved.

"Water," they shaped. "Water."

Shale thrust his hand into his pocket and withdrew a small flask of brandy.

"Drink," he commanded, and held the precious spirit to the other's parched mouth.

A new light came into Lord Anderley's eyes as the warming fluid thrilled him. Gently, Shale reached over and cut the stirrup leather, letting the twisted foot sink softly to the ground.

"I—I thank you, friend," muttered the injured man, "though 'tis of little use."

"How so, m'lord?"

"Because I—I am not long for this world, Shale."

"Nay, m'lord, dost think you could let me bear thee to Riverhead where help can be gotten?"

Anderley's battered head moved feebly.

" 'Tis useless, man," he whispered, "I have but a few moments left, and these I would spend in talk with you."

Shale knew that the man was speaking the truth. His head was badly wounded, but it was not this that was leading death towards him.

A pool of blood dyed the green grass red where it had trickled to the ground from a bullet-wound in Anderley's left side.

"Aye," he whispered, " 'tis that accursed bullet that has finished me."

Shale's mind went back to the scene in the

taproom of the "Whyte Hart" when the ill-assorted pair, Simon and Benjamin, had sat by the fire.

"M'lord," he said, "was it the rogues I warned you against?"

Anderley's eyes gleamed.

" 'Tis like enough," he muttered, "but I cannot tell. The assassins fired from the side of the road, and hit me ere I knew what had happened."

Shale gave him another drink and momentarily strengthened, he went on talking in halting, jerky sentences, gasping heavily for breath between each of them.

"I fell from my horse, but my foot caught in my stirrup and so I was dragged—battered—and kicked—ah, God give me breath—along the road to this spot, to which the brute wandered in search of grass. And here I was when I came to my senses a short while since."

He stopped and motioned Shale to give him more brandy. His face was growing grayish in its pallor, and it seemed as if the shadow of death was descending upon it.

"Quick, man, come closer," he gasped. "What I have to say is of vital import to thee."

"To me?" asked Shale in surprise. "Nay, surely not to me, m'lord," and he wondered if Anderley's mind was wandering.

"Aye, to you man," muttered the dying noble.
"Hearken to me now."

He made a last desperate effort and raised his
head.

"Shale, I know full well who hath brought
my death about."

"Who, m'lord?"

"Sir Humphrey Clayville."

Shale started.

"Surely you are mistaken, m'lord," he said.
"Were you not to wed his niece?"

A wry smile twisted itself upon Anderley's
lips.

"Aye, and for that very reason he desired my
death—since if I did not wed the Lady Gloria
before the end of this year, her great wealth left
her by her father passes to Sir Humphrey."

A grim light dawned in Shale's eyes. If this
were true, there surely was good reason why Sir
Humphrey should desire the death of Lord Anderley.

"My father was her father's dearest friend,"
gasped the dying man, "and it was the wish of
both that we, their offspring, should wed. The
better to achieve this end, m'lady and I were
reared well apart, that our hearts might waken
of a sudden when we met. Yet so we were

practically betrothed before my father died five
years ago."

He fell back exhausted, and lay a while gasping on the mossy sward.

"Go on, m'lord," said Shale, plying the
brandy flask to his lips once again.

Anderley made a grand effort.

"Sir Hubert Clayville, m'lady's father, died
a few months a-gone, and in his will disposing of
his heritage, he made it a condition that his
daughter, Gloria, should wed with me, failing
which Sir Humphrey would inherit the estates."

Again he gasped and again he recovered his
breath sufficiently to proceed, though his voice
was but the merest whisper now.

"And now my murderer will win unless—unless——"

"Well? well?" asked Shale, bending over him
anxiously.

The dying man looked up at him.

"Friend," he whispered, "wilt promise me a
dying favor?"

Shale bowed his head.

"If 'tis vengeance, m'lord, 'twere better in
God's hands, but if 'tis anything that does not
mean the spilling of blood I will promise you it
shall be done."

" 'Tis vengeance sweet and cunning," whispered Anderley, "but calling not for bloodshed, friend. Wilt promise? Wilt take thy oath?"

Shale breathed deeply.

"Aye," he muttered.

A look almost of happiness came into the dying man's face.

"My boon is this"—his voice sounded far away—"take my place and live my life as it ought to have been lived."

Shale started to his feet bewildered.

"But, my lord, 'twere imposture! 'twere robbery."

Anderley looked up at him fiercely.

" 'Twere justice and vengeance," he cried aloud, raising himself on his elbow by a last tremendous effort. " 'Twere giving the Lady Gloria her just portion. 'Twere cheating a fox of its prey. And you've promised—aye, on oath."

He fell back overcome and Shale, knowing that death, black death, was stealing away his soul, bent closer to him and took his hand in his own.

The weary eyes opened for the last time.

"My friend—keep—thy oath, and you'll do no wrong—for mark you the likeness between us. It—is not there without a reason, for you are—he—who—ah!"

The whispering voice trailed away into the distance, and the poor head fell back.

And with a soft sigh—almost a sigh of content —Lord Anderley passed to a better world.

WHEN JOHN SHALE KEEPS HIS OATH

SHALE knelt a long time beside the stiffening form of the dead nobleman.

He was bewildered. This dramatic climax to the strange adventures of the past hours was almost more than he could cope with. He felt as one in a dream, and every now and again he pressed his hand in dazed fashion to his forehead.

What had he promised this man? Gradually it came back to him.

He had promised to take his place as Lord Anderley. What did that involve?

His pondering mind realized that it meant him taking up the position in the world held by the dead man. It meant him having unlimited wealth with which to gratify his every whim. It meant him being avenged in truly cunning fashion upon the man who had been the means of landing him in this plight, the man whose hired bailiffs had driven him from the farm whereon he had lived the happiest years of his life. It meant the gratifying of this dead man's

66

desire. It meant all these things and many more, but most of all, it meant the granting of that which he had hardly dared to hope.

It meant that he would meet again the girl who had come so strangely into his life as that fateful morning dawned. Aye, and not only meet her, for was she not betrothed to Lord Anderley, and would he not be, as far as any one knew, Lord Anderley. It meant she would become his wife.

A strange wild look came into honest John Shale's blue eyes.

"God in heaven," he moaned, "save me from temptation."

But still the form of that sweet maid loomed before him, and again he saw her as he had seen her first, clasped close in his arms, her head against his breast, panting like a fawn in fear.

"And I have given my oath," he said aloud. "My word of honor, which I ne'er have broken yet."

He staggered to his feet, and with hands pressed to his temples, stood in silence.

The dead man's last words came back to his bewildered brain.

"Mark you the likeness between us. It is not there without a reason."

What could he have meant. Had Anderley been a follower of fate, and believed that 'twas destined that—that he, Shale, should fill his shoes, or was there something further. He could not tell.

"In truth, I know not what to do," he cried at last, throwing out his hands in sheer despair.

"Zookers, 'twere simple enough. Mount you your horse, and let us for Orpington. We've tarried in these parts long enough, m'lord."

Shale looked round thunderstruck.

There at the edge of the glade stood Peter.

He had a bloody handkerchief bound round his head—his face and clothes were bespattered with mud, and he seemed to sway a little as he stood—but withal it was Peter.

"Ah, Peter," said Shale, slowly, " 'tis truly good to see you, and know that you are not dead."

"And 'tis good to me to know that you are here, and safe and well, m'lord," quoth Peter. There was a barely imperceptible pause before the last word.

Shale looked him full in the face. All his old coolness had returned to him. All his wonderful self-control was again at his will's command.

"You know me well, Peter," he said, still gazing steadily into the man's eyes.

Peter returned the stare stolidly.

"Aye! I know you well, m'lord."

Shale looked down at the green sward thoughtfully.

"Then do you not mark any change in me?" he said.

"None, m'lord."

"How long have you been standing there, Peter?"

A pause—then:

"But long enough to recognize you as—m'lord."

" 'Twere hard to do so then."

" 'Tis hard to see at all when blood is trickling in the eyes."

"And hard to hear as well."

"Aye!—m'lord—there is a constant buzzing in mine ears."

"You mark the scene within this little glade?"

"I do, m'lord."

"In all its points?"

"Aye, m'lord."

"You mark yonder—yonder heap—upon the ground?"

"I do, m'lord."

"Dost recognize the—the face of he who lies there?"

" 'Tis a poor mutilated face, m'lord. Methinks, 'twere hard to make the features out."

"You know who he is."

"He is a dead man, m'lord, and may God rest his soul."

"Amen."

A long silence, then——

"Hast ever seen these clothes he wears, before, friend Peter?"

"Aye, m'lord."

"Where?"

"Upon the back of he who owns them."

"And that is?"

"Lord Anderley, m'lord."

"And is he here just now?"

"He is."

"And which of us is he?"

"Thou art he, m'lord."

Shale emitted a deep sigh and turned away.

"M'lord."

"Aye, Peter."

Shale uttered the words before he realized that by doing so he was acknowledging the title. It amazed him to realize that he so readily had become accustomed to it.

"Wilt suffer me to lead thy mount to the roadway, sire?"

John gave a gesture of indifference.

"Do what you will, man, 'tis in thy hands."

Peter grasped the horse's bridle, then turned to the master he had adopted.

"We await you, m'lord."

Shale looked down at the silent figure on the green.

"He will be buried, m'lord—where none shall disturb his peace."

"You mean?"

"M'lord will leave that to me."

Again a long pause. At last Shale silently walked to the edge of the wood, and Peter led the horse crashing through the bushes. And Shale was so occupied with his thoughts that he forgot all about his tall, furry hat lying in the glade.

At the roadway they found the serving man's mount gently munching the sweet, dewy grass by the side of the woods.

Peter crossed to it, and unstrapped a blanket which was rolled across the pommel of the saddle.

"Wilt await me here a space, m'lord?"

Shale nodded his understanding, and the man disappeared in the direction of the glade.

In a few minutes he returned carrying the rich riding coat which Anderley had worn, but which was now covered with mud and wet with dew. Still its richness was apparent, and Peter held it up.

"M'lord!"

Shale shuddered.

"Nay, Peter, I'll ride without it."

"Zookers, m'lord," quoth Peter. "To proceed in such clothes as these were to make idle gossip."

" 'Tis a dead man's coat, Peter, gossip or no gossip. I'll not put it across my back."

Peter sighed.

"Then I'll sling it across your saddle, m'lord. P'raps 'twill serve as well."

"Aye, sling it across the saddle, man, but put it so 'tis behind me. I want not to have it flaunt me i' the face."

They mounted and rode down the highway into the village of Riverhead.

At the crossroads they drew up and Peter looked at his master.

"Methinks 'twere better, m'lord, an' we go first to thine own manor at Bessels Green ere proceeding to Sir Humphrey Clayville's place at Orpington. 'Tis here the road branches off."

"An' thou wilt, Peter," said Shale, and they swerved round and started the last short mile to Anderley Hall.

As they rode, Peter opened a conversation and they spoke in this way:

"You must be tired, m'lord."

"I am that, Peter, man."

"You'll rest awhile at Anderley Hall."

"True. I will most certain see to that. But

Peter, my brain is somewhat tired, and these strange events have rendered my thoughts of things that have taken place but hazy. Tell me, man, from whence have we come?"

"Zookers, m'lord, and I do not wonder at your daze. So now will I give you a short survey of some of the things of greatest import to you, the better that you may grasp the purpose of your mission here."

"Go on, man!"

"Well, m'lord, you know well I have held your confidence in most things."

"And always will, Peter."

"Thank you, m'lord. Well as I was a-saying, you confided to me that you were journeying to Orpington to woo the Lady Gloria Clayville for your wife. And even now you are betrothed to her."

"Of that I am aware."

"And, moreover, 'tis of urgent need that you should wed her, m'lord."

"For why, Peter?"

"Zookers, m'lord, because your lavish expenditure and extravagant ways have sadly depleted the coffers of your estates."

"And so I am extravagant, eh, Peter. Tell me, man, am I also considered a heavy drinker."

"One of the deepest in Paris, m'lord, from

whence we have just journeyed; after five long
months there."

"Ah, methought 'twas Paris. But that
reminds me. Am I also somewhat of a dissolute
and lustful nature."

"It hath so been said, m'lord. And in Paris
your name was something of a byword in that
respect. So numerous were your amours that
on no fewer than six occasions you had the seconds of maddened lovers awaiting upon you."

Shale frowned.

"My heritage is a somewhat mixed one, Peter.
Its blessings and its curses are well intermingled.
Tell me, did I slay any of those indignant lovers."

"Three you left dead upon the dueling ground,
and three were sadly wounded. 'Twas well nigh
time you left Paris, for 'twas becoming very
warm for you, m'lord."

Shale's frown deepened.

"Three deaths to my credit, or rather discredit
already, and all lovers' brawls. Ugh, Peter, I
feel me somewhat sick."

Peter remained silent for a few minutes, then:

"Aye, 'twere foolishness on thy part, m'lord,
but, zookers, methinks you've gathered more
sense by now."

"Nay, Peter, I think I'm fast losing my senses.
But proceed, man. What next?"

"There's little else, m'lord, except that you must wed M'lady Gloria Clayville ere the end of this year, or she will be disinherited, and your chances of recuperating your depleted estates will be sadly spoiled."

"So I am to wed m'lady and share her gold, eh? 'Tis a mercenary scheme. And what does m'lady say to this?"

"Zookers, m'lord, therein is the difficulty, for she hath written you thrice telling you she'll have nought to do with any dissolute gallant who hankers after her purse. And in this attitude she is supported by her uncle, Sir Humphrey Clayville, whose motive is plain, since he will inherit m'lady's money should she not become your bride. And 'twere well to beware of Sir Humphrey, m'lord, for he hath a plotting way with him, and methinks he hath already been behind a dastardly attempt to rid the world of you."

"Aye, I feel it in my bones that 'twas he who engineered that ambush, Peter, and doubtless he will yet make another attempt."

Peter swore loud and deep, and his brow was black as thunder.

After another silence, Shale spoke again.

"Dost remember yon wench at the 'Whyte Hart,' Peter?"

"Aye, m'lord," answered the servant in a very low voice.

"Where was it I met her before, Peter?"

" 'Twas in your own house, Anderley Hall, where she was serving maid, m'lord. Methinks you were somewhat foolish in that instance, m'lord, but 'twere your own affair."

Another long silence.

"I have it in my mind, Peter, that the burdens of this my new estate are likely to prove too heavy for me."

"Zookers, m'lord. These are but little things to such as you. One does not call them burdens, for your shoulders are broad and your heart is strong."

"Aye, strong, Peter, but not overwilling."

Peter looked at him with a confident smile.

"You'll never shirk a burden or an adventure, m'lord, an' I know you right."

Shale took a deep breath.

"Nay, Peter, never. And now enough of these regrets. I've put my hand to the plow, Peter, and I'll ne'er let go till the field is turned."

"Zookers, m'lord, 'tis good to hear you say it. And remember I will be by your side to help you guide it."

Shale held out his hand, and the two men clasped warmly.

Now the great gate of Anderley Hall loomed up before them and, as they halted, the gatekeeper, an old man, well nigh blind, hobbled out.

"And who would have entrance to Anderley Hall?" he croaked.

Shale made an imperious gesture that thrilled Peter with satisfaction.

"Who, knave, who but your lord and master? Open at once to Lord Anderley, of Anderley Hall."

The old man tottered to the gate shouting welcome and pleading pardon for the delay.

And as he did so a young forester, some little distance up the wide drive, caught sight of the horsemen and turning ran swiftly towards the great mansion house to spread the good news to the servants that their lord had returned from France, and was even now at the gate.

HOW A FARMER KISSES A LADY'S HAND

THE sun's searching rays peeped through a maze of tree tops, and discovering a wide lattice window, jutting out from the timbered walls of Anderley Hall. danced and darted merrily towards it.

And passing through the tiny window panes, they lit up the room beyond with their wonderful soft light, and bathed it in mellow warmth.

And the honeysuckle and climbing roses, clinging to the walls around that self same lattice, opened their tender petals to the life-giving rays, and breathed out their fragrance on the early morning air.

The soft enchanting scent was wafted into the room and mingled with the sunshine among the hanging draperies of blue and gold, and among the tapestry of delicate texture.

Stealing across the great four-poster bed, the sun rays discovered the frank, open face of a sleeping man, a face crowned with dark crisp hair.

And like little elves they danced upon the

closed eyelids till they quivered with the shock, and the soft fragrance tickled the nostrils of the man and teased them with its deliciousness.

And the eyes opened wide, and gazed out through the lattice, and the nostrils breathed to the full the honeysuckle and roses, and the ears harkened to the wild birds singing in the trees.

And thus, with a deep sigh, John Shale awoke to his first real day as a proud noble.

All the previous day and all night he had lain him asleep, and the servants stepped quietly in the manor, for m'lord was fatigued after his long journey from Paris, and must not be disturbed.

And now as he awakened he looked about him in perplexity and wonderment.

Then slowly the wonderful events that had taken place on that fateful night when he had walked along the London Road, came to him.

He leaned back and sighed contentedly. Any misgivings that might have leapt to his mind were banished at once by the delicious environment in which he now found himself.

He felt that until this moment he had not known what comfort was—he had not realized what 'twas to live. He did not feel at all strange amidst his gorgeous surroundings—just filled with a sweet sense of contentment.

He did not trouble to ponder upon the diffi-

culties with which he would be brought face to
face in the days to come—aye—even within the
next few hours. He put all thoughts of that ilk
from him, and for the moment reveled in the
novelty of his content and gazed dreamily at the
carved ceiling.

He was a lord—a noble—one of the chosen
few—one of the lucky ones. His future welfare
was assured, his days of distress were behind
him (at least so he told himself) and only pleasure lay in front.

And so he lay and dreamed of joys to come,
and into his dreams little soft curls of hair
seemed to be woven, and they were yellow curls
and crowned the head of a sweet girlish face
with eyes of brown, or black, or violet (for the
life of him he could not tell which), eyes which
once had looked up at him pleadingly, but which
now seemed to hold a roguish twinkle.

At first he wondered vaguely who the maid
was, then quite suddenly it came to him that she
was, of course, the Lady Gloria Clayville, and
he smiled at his own denseness and sighed again.
For he remembered that she was betrothed to
Lord Anderley, this maid of his dreams, and was
not he Lord Anderley?

He saw his face reflected in an oval mirrored

glass set in a white enameled frame hanging above the mantel, and he spoke to himself.

"Good morning, Lord Anderley. You've slept well, 'tis plain. And little wonder, for on pillows such as these, methinks you'd sleep a month and ne'er wake. So there you lie, smug-faced and well content with the turn events have taken in your favor, and with no thought of surrendering up these comforts new acquired. Aye, well nigh forgetting already that you are of plebeian birth and that, instead of lord of these estates and master of this great manor, you are simply and only John Shale—a sham—aye, a mere sham."

He paused and looked quizzically at himself.

"And yet withal, methinks you'd much prefer to be a sham lord than genuine farmer, for how could a poor penniless tiller of the soil dare to aspire to the hand of the lady who is soon to become the bride of a sham lord. I'faith whatever difficulties beset your new estate, it hath its compensations, John—er, I mean Lord Geoffrey. Zounds, but I'll have to practice the saying of my new name, or I'll be blurting out the one I've left behind."

He rose from the bed and crossing to the window, opened wide the lattice, and gazed out.

A beauteous sight met his gaze. First there was a green lawn fresh with the morning dew and bordered by a delightful rose garden with winding paths and raised beds of every conceivable shape. At the foot of this garden was an avenue of creeping flowers twining o'er a long rustic arch, and this avenue led to a quaint little bower covered with roses and flowers of every hue.

Now seeing this bower, John Shale was imbued with an unaccountable desire to view it closer. Perhaps he was as yet unable to completely forget that he had trained to be a farmer and, as such, was naturally interested in such beauteous horticulture as was here displayed.

Be that as it may, the desire was there, and being now Lord Anderley, and no longer Farmer Shale, desires were made but to be granted.

Accordingly, he looked around the room for something with which to cover his long, powerful shanks, and lighted upon the old homespun breeches which lay neatly folded upon a chair beside a host of gorgeous attire, more suitable for the person of a lord.

So John Shale forgot for the moment what he had been so pleased to think a few minutes before, namely, that he was a noble ostensibly of high birth, and donned his ancient breeches and coarse wool hose and cotton shirt, and gently pushing open his bedroom door, crept him silently along the soft-carpeted corridors and down the great bannistered staircase, and past the many entrances to the huge reception rooms, and across the hall, and through the open door, and out into the rose garden.

He stood for a moment looking round him and breathing the fresh morning air, then he walked slowly down the winding flowered archway towards the bower of roses at its end.

Now turning a sudden bend he came upon it.

And he stared into it in sheer amaze.

For there, kneeling on the ground with her face buried in her hands and her golden curls shining in the sun, was a girl.

And she was weeping.

She had not heard him approach, and he stood gazing down at her entranced for a full minute.

Then something made her lower her hands from her face, and her eyes caught sight of his great coarse shoes with their rusty steel buckles.

"Oh," she gasped, and her eyes rose slowly upwards, taking in first his hose, then his breeches and coarse shirt wide open at the neck, showing his brawny throat, and with sleeves dangling loosely from the elbows, and last of all his tanned face and serious blue eyes gazing calmly down at her.

"Oh," she gasped again, and sprang to her feet,

at the same time dabbing the crystal tears from her eyes by a skillfully concealed maneuver with a lace kerchief.

"Oh," she gasped yet again.

M'lord bowed.

" 'Tis the third 'Oh,' madame, and never a greeting for me."

She laughed now, quite forgetful of the fact that but a moment before she had been in tears.

"Why! 'Tis my hero of the fight in the highway a night ago. In very sooth I crave forgiveness for not greeting you 'ere now, but indeed you came upon me so unexpected that I had little time to say aught but 'oh.' "

"And yet you'd time to wipe away a number o' tears, m'lady."

She frowned to think that her skillfully contrived motion had not escaped this man's keen eye.

"Tears, sir, on a morn like this? Methinks your mind is over melancholy."

Shale laughed.

"Faith, no, madame. I'm anything but that. There's no mistaking a woman in tears and in truth it grieves me sore to think that you should weep. Wil't tell me why?"

She raised her little nose pertly.

"And why should I, sir? 'Tis true indeed you

gave me aid when I was pursued; but after all, your aid served me but little, since I was recaptured in the end and dragged back here to further undergo the process of being bent to the will of a most determined lady."

"Eh!" gasped Shale. "A lady say you. In sooth, who is she?"

She looked at him quizzically.

"My, what a cross-examination to put a maid through at this hour o' the morn. Prithee, tell me what do you here?"

He almost seemed surprised that she had not known who he was, then it slowly dawned upon him that the Lady Gloria Clayville had never seen Lord Anderley, and beyond all doubt this was the Lady Gloria.

He glanced down at his ill-kept clothes. Belike she took him for some stable hand or gardening churl. Well, there was no harm done an' she did.

He laughed.

"I'faith, ma'am, I came here partly on the back of a good horse, but mostly by the help of these big feet o' mine."

"And by what right are you here?" she demanded.

He laughed again.

"An' it please you, fair lady, might I ask you the same?"

She frowned, and her little foot tapped the ground.

"I'm here because 'tis here I've been since I was carried back on that black night when I encountered you, sir."

He rubbed his chin thoughtfully.

"Methinks you said something about a lady, ma'am."

"Indeed, I did, sir, but 'twere not my desire to converse of my affairs with m'lord's groom."

A wistful look came into his eyes at her words.

"Ah! m'lady," he said, " 'twere not in keeping with your eyes to hurt so deep as that."

She bent and plucked a rose that he might not see the color in her cheeks.

He watched her for a moment, then silently turned away.

"I—I'm sorry," she said softly, "wilt forgive me, friend?"

She held out her hand, and he bowed and kissed it.

"And now," she said, looking at him quizzically again, "an' you're not—not what I called you, prithee, tell me who and what you are?"

He stood back and gazed at her a long time.

And as he looked there sounded a sudden ex-

cited voice behind him, accompanied by the shuffling of clumsy feet, and Peter rounded the bend
in the archway and came upon them.

"Ah! m'lord," he gasped. "I have been searching everywhere for you. I thought—I thought
that you had—had—had—zookers, m'lady."

But now m'lady was not looking at him. Her
eyes were fixed upon the face of Shale.

"M'lord!" she gasped. "Did'st say m'lord.
Then—then you are Lord Anderley."

Shale bowed his head.

She gave a little cry and tore at her hand
where he had touched it with his lips.

"Ugh!" she gasped, her voice throbbing with
repugnance. " 'Twere better an'—an' you were
but—a groom."

Then raising her head high in the air she
pushed past the two men, and strode towards the
house.

And, watching her, John Shale sighed deeply,
while Peter emitted an astounded "zookers"!

CALLS FOR PROMPT ACTION ON JOHN'S PART

SHALE looked at Peter at last.

"Peter, my man, can'st tell me how she got here?"

Peter shuffled uncomfortably.

"I—I could not say for sure, m'lord."

M'lord eyed him narrowly.

"Ah, well, venture a guess. Mayhap you'll hit the real manner of it an' you try."

Again Peter shuffled.

"'Twere a matter of much surprise to me to find her in the garden, m'lord."

Shale gave a gesture of impatience.

"Zounds, man, wilt answer me, and not dilly dally with the question."

"Aye, aye, sire," gasped Peter quickly—" 'twere like this. I'd promised not to tell you she was here."

"So ho!" quoth m'lord, "an' who did'st give this promise to, man?"

"To—to your aunt, sire."

Shale nearly jumped into the air with surprise.

"My aunt, d'ye say. Have I an aunt then, rogue?"

"Aye, m'lord, that in truth you have, sire— aye, in very truth."

"In very truth, say you. Humph! tell me, man, is she a—a most determined lady?"

Peter looked up eagerly.

"You've hit it, m'lord, 'tis exactly what she is, sire. Most determined, sire; in fact, sire, pardon the liberty I may seem to take with your aunt—I should say damned determined, m'lord."

"M'm!" mused Shale. "Here's a pretty kettle o' fish, Peter. All these twenty-four hours have I been in this, my own house, and never heard till now I had an aunt. Faith, 'tis lucky an' I mentioned the matter, else, meeting her, I might have thought she was a housekeeper or something of that ilk, and had my ears soundly boxed for my pains. Aye, you're a pretty schemer, indeed, you rascal."

Peter blushed and looked down at his big feet with a sigh—then after a silence.

"May I venture to remind you, m'lord, that you are not dressed with dignity beseeming your station."

Shale looked down at his breeches and hose and then chuckled.

" 'Tis a clever retally, man. Faith, there's two of us. I fear we are but poor conspirators."

"Wilt please to go into the house and dress now, m'lord? Your clothes are set out awaiting you."

Shale laughed.

"Aye, Peter, in a minute—in a minute—but first you must tell me why you promised my—my aunt that you would not tell me the Lady Gloria was here. And how did she get here anyway?"

Peter sighed.

"I had no choice but promise to keep the secret, m'lord. You see when your aunt makes up her mind to a thing there is never any choice, sire."

"Go on, man. What was the object o't?"

" 'Tis simple, sire. You see, m'lady Genevieve (that is your aunt's name), hath the affairs o' the family deep at heart, and she is determined to let nothing come in the way of your wedding with M'lady Gloria, and so she hath kept m'lady here beside her, she told me, for nigh a week past, lest her uncle, Sir Humphrey Clayville, should spirit her away, and also for fear that she should fly herself from meeting you."

"Fly from meeting me, man. What is there to fear in me?"

"Nothing, m'lord, at least nothing for a woman

to fear, but M'lady Gloria hath, it seems, a will of her own, though so has the Lady Genevieve, who is a—a——"

"A damned determined woman, Peter," put in Sale.

"Zookers, aye, m'lord, for she hath kept the Lady Gloria here in spite of the fact that, on the very night we tarried at the 'Whyte Hart,' the Lady Gloria bribed a coachman to drive her in a chaise to Folkestone. The Lady Genevieve missed her and sent seven stout fellows well mounted to fetch her back, and fetch her back they did, though not till after a desperate struggle with some churl who did befriend her on the highway."

"Go on, Peter," quoth Shale, " 'tis a mighty interesting narrative."

"Well, m'lord, Lady Genevieve's idea was to arrange a surprise for both the Lady Gloria and you, and she was preparing to stage a most romantic meeting this very evening. Thus she deemed it wise to take me into her confidence, and impressed me sorely with the secrecy o't. And now you've met the Lady Gloria, and the saints above know what the Lady Genevieve will say to me in her wrath. I shiver me to think on't."

"She seems a truly wonderful woman, Peter. I'faith, I'd like to meet her."

They were walking slowly towards the house when suddenly Peter grasped his master's arm.

"You have your wish, master, for here she is. Faith, I must be off, sire, to prepare your clothes."

Shale looked at him anxiously.

"Nay, man, you've already said that they are ready."

Peter flushed.

"Aye, sire, but there's a small matter I had forgotten," he said desperately. "An' it please you, m'lord, I will be off."

Shale smiled sardonically.

"Go then, Peter, go. But harken, man—you have not the courage of a mouse."

Which scolding Peter accepted most meekly and hurried up the flowered archway, just reaching the corner where it joined the path in time to avoid the Lady Genevieve, before she entered it.

She approached the new Lord Anderley with a serene sailing motion.

She was a little woman, slim, with shrewd, sharp features, and a keen look in her pale blue eyes. Her hair was white, and was pulled primly back beneath a lace cap which she wore.

She was clad in a long gray gown with large

red geraniums painted on it. They were very red geraniums, and their redness was accentuated by the fact that in the center of every four blooms there was a blue one. Shale never remembered having seen blue geraniums before, and he found himself fascinated by them now.

It was difficult, in fact, to keep his eyes off them.

The Lady Genevieve walked straight up to him and surveyed him for a few minutes with critical eye.

He bowed stiffly, and she returned the salutation with an equally stiff obeisance.

"Good morning, Geoffrey."

"Good morning, aunt."

"Aunt, dear—Geoffrey," she corrected him. "You forget my teaching before you went to Paris."

"Aunt, dear," repeated Shale soberly.

"And is this the fashion of garb in which you take your early morning walk in Paris?" she went on, indicating his coarse clothes.

He flushed.

"No aunt—dear, but I'm not in Paris now, you know."

"No reason why you should go about like a stable hand, Geoffrey. Besides, I have a particular desire for you to be careful with your dress."

He elevated his brows.

"Yes—aunt—dear. And what is it?"

She frowned.

"I'm not telling," she said sharply, as if annoyed at having said so much. "You'll learn soon enough."

He smiled.

"Is it because the Lady Gloria Clayville is here?"

She looked at him in quick surprise.

"How did you guess?" she snapped out.

He laughed now.

"Ah, then it is so, aunt—dear. Well I guessed because I have just been speaking with her."

Aunt Genevieve gave a little squeal.

"Catch me, Geoffrey. Catch me. I swoon. I swoon."

He looked at her in alarm.

"Nay, madam, I pray thee, control thyself. I beg of thee——"

But the little lady had already swooned and, taking a dainty little step towards him, she flopped softly into his arms.

He stood looking down at her in consternation for a moment. What to do, he did not know. Never had he been in such a predicament.

Suddenly he bethought himself of Peter. Peter would know—he seemed to know everything.

"Hi—Peter—Peter!" he called.

There was a sudden startled movement in his arms and the form of Aunt Genevieve became less limp.

"Hi—Peter!" he called again, and she opened her eyes and looked at him indignantly.

"And where are your fine Paris manners, Geoffrey?" she gasped. "Is this how the frog-eaters treat a poor woman in a swoon?"

"I' faith, I am greatly eased to hear you speak, aunt—dear," Shale essayed, " 'tis the first time I had a lady faint in my arms so."

She struggled to her feet, and eyed him askance.

"The first time"—she echoed. "Geoffrey, do not try to deceive me. An' even half the tales I've heard of you in Paris be true, 'tis well for you you're back here at Bessels Green again. I've never breathed easy since you went for fear you would elope with some French chit of a girl and forget your duty—your bounden duty to your family."

Shale thought of the six duels and the three dead men that had resulted, and he sighed. 'Twere well to say nothing, but to accept the scolding in silence lest she should raise the matter

of these fatal amours his predecessor had contracted.

"But you lead me from the point, Geoffrey.
Did I hear aright when you said you'd met Lady
Gloria Clayville?"

"Yes, aunt—dear," he replied.

"Where?"

"Here in this garden—in yon very bower in
fact."

She looked at him in horror.

"And you in these clothes, Geoffrey?"

He looked at them ruefully.

"In truth, they are a trifle worse o' wear," he
said, "but they've served me well."

"Served you well, indeed. I should say they
have, but they look as if they'd served a farmer
well instead."

Shale flushed.

"Faith, and they have."

"What's that," she asked sharply.

"I said faith and they have been good breeches,
aunt—dear," he hurriedly explained in a meek
tone.

"And what do you think er—how do you like
—er—what is your opinion of Lady Gloria?" she
asked in softer voice.

He looked down at the roses.

"She is a charming lady," he said fervently.

To his amazement, the Lady Genevieve suddenly reached up and kissed him.

"Why—the poor boy blushes like a maid," she laughed next instant. "And when did you learn to turn red when I kissed you, Geoffrey?"

He seemed very embarrassed.

"B—but this moment, m'lady, er—er—aunt, dear."

Again she laughed.

" 'Tis plain you are in love, Geoffrey."

He stared at her in amazement.

"In love, ma'am?"

"Aye, Geoffrey, in love and indeed 'tis that which pleaseth me so that I needs must kiss you!"

"But you're mistaken ma'am," gasped Shale. "I've only met the lady twice—er, I mean once."

She looked at him sharply.

"Did you say once or twice, Geoffrey?"

He rose to the occasion.

"I said both, aunt—dear, but I only meant to say once."

"Ah, well," she observed, "no matter, 'tis plain you are smitten, and thus much of my hopes are realized. There only remains the girl to deal with now."

"Aye," quoth Shale. "There's the girl."

Again that sharp, keen look.

"Did she seem to be glad to see you?"

He looked at her thoughtfully.

"She did, ma'am, and then again she didn't."

"Don't speak to me in riddles, Geoffrey. I suppose you mean she had no liking for you till you told her who you were. In truth she must have thought you a stable hand at first."

"You are right, ma'am, and you're wrong."

She frowned, and stamped her foot.

"No riddles, boy, d'ye hear me. What mean you?"

Shale smiled.

"I mean, aunt, that——"

"Aunt, dear, please.

"Aunt—dear," he corrected. "I mean that at first M'lady Gloria seemed pleased to see me, but when she found I was Lord Anderley, she flew from me in dire disgust."

Again the little old lady frowned.

"The minx," she muttered. "Of course, 'tis plain she is but self-willed. Because she was betrothed to you by her father and because her inheritance depends upon her wedding you, she must, of course, determine not to do so."

"That is plain," agreed Shale heartily, but regretted his words immediately, for, in an instant, the lady had rounded on him again.

"Plain, indeed. And who made it plain, sir.

Your very self and none other. By your numberless amours in Paris and by the reckless manner in which you made your name a byeword of the countryside with your deep drinking and fast living. 'Tis no surprise that the Lady Gloria spurned you."

Shale stood with bowed head for a long time while Aunt Genevieve bit her lips with regret for having said so much in her fury.

"Aye, ma'am, you're right," he said at last, speaking in a low voice. " 'Twere indeed a sin to let the mire o' my loathsomeness besmirch the beauty o' her presence."

Tears started to the old lady's eyes—tears that had something of glad surprise in them. 'Twas fine to feel the boy—her boy, as she liked to think him—had still some good left in him.

"Nay, do not grieve so, Geoffrey," she said softly. "After all, thou art a man and men are granted much licence. Besides, she hath been foolish herself, though not to justify the stories that are told. For she is very beautiful, and the penalty of beauty is always the jealousy of other women. There is one noxious story in very special which I'd warn you to heed not, and that is that she did fence with an——"

She stopped suddenly, for Shale's hand was uplifted in a gesture of reproof.

"Nay, ma'am, nay. Speak it not. Such babble is not worthy of thy breath. I bid you good morn, aunt—dear."

And as he strode a-down the path, his handsome head held high, the Lady Genevieve laughed a queer little laugh and whispered to herself.

"My boy—my own dear boy. He hath wonderfully improved of late. These stories must be lies."

THE TALL FURRY HAT IS RESURRECTED

A FTER breakfasting alone in his room, Shale had a sad struggle getting into his fine new clothes. They fitted him well enough, but the jacket of apple green silk broidered with gold lace was a trifle tight across the shoulders.

"Egad, but I look a mighty important personage now, Peter," he said, as he surveyed his handsome figure in the long dressing glass. "What with green silk trousers, jacket and hose and Brussels lace cravat and gold waistcoat and red-heeled shoes, I am a veritable dandy. Nay, Peter, man," as the latter approached with a big powder puff in his hand, "there is enough o' that upon my wig. Faith, I've as much flour about me as would bake a full-sized loaf."

He accepted his black velvet three-cornered hat and gold-knobbed staff, then stood back for a final survey.

"Well, Peter," he said. "Am I more like myself in this attire?"

Peter stared at him in open admiration.

"Zookers, m'lord," he gasped, "you're the very spirit of—of yourself."

Shale took out his purse and tossed him a guinea in most approved fashion.

"Did I do it well," he asked.

Peter grinned.

"Aye, m'lord. But you'll improve still more with practice."

"You rascal, man," laughed Shale. "Now methinks I will take me a walk around my estate, and see if I can gather the accustom o' it."

So saying he strode from the dressing room, and descended the wide staircase.

Half way down the stairs he was arrested by the sound of a deep singing voice drifting in through an open casement.

> I love the hunt,
> I love the hounds,
> I love my horse to carry me.
>> But most of all
>> I love sweet Poll,
> The maid that's going to marry me.

> Heigh-o, heigh-o, but I am a weary soul,
>> A-grooming horses all day long,
>> And singing of a lovesick song,
> Which makes me feel more dole,
> Which makes me feel more dole.

The song ceased, and gave place to a steady hissing noise.

Thrusting his head through the casement, John found that he was looking out into the stable yard in the rear of the Hall.

Seated on an upturned pail with the cobbles around him strewn with harness was a stable hand hard at work polishing a bridle the while he hissed like a persistent bee.

There would have been nothing unusual about him had it not been for one thing.

Around his head was a bandage, and it supported a big beef steak which was plastered over his left eye. Around the beef steak the flies were buzzing merrily to the not inconsiderable annoyance of the man.

Suddenly he leapt high into the air with a yell of pain, and looked furiously about him.

"That's the second time within two minutes summat 'as struck me bandage," he spluttered, rasping out an oath. "There's summat behind this 'ere, there is."

He cast his one free eye around the stable yard, and an exclamation of satisfaction escaped him.

Stooping he picked up something from the ground.

"A pea," he ejaculated. "Aha—now somebody must 'ave shied that at me."

He looked around him furiously.

"Come out," he roared. "Come out, who ever ye are, an' I'll duck ye in the horsetrough."

There was no response, whereupon he roared again.

"Show yer head ye coward, an' I'll split it open for ye. A hittin' of a poor wounded man wot can't see ye. Come out into the open, and I'll bung up both yer eyes."

There was a ripple of soft musical laughter.

A curly, yellow head peeped from behind a huge water butt, and a dainty hand raised a long tube to pouted lips. Then another pea sped upon its tantalizing errand.

But now the stable hand seemed to have lost all his fearsomeness, and instead of attempting to carry out any of his dire threats, contented himself with standing still and pulling his fore-lock awkwardly.

Lady Gloria advanced to within three yards of him, and raised her blowpipe again.

"Nay, m'lady," groaned the man, "I pray you, 'tis torture to hit me bandage."

She laughed her rippling laugh again.

" 'Tis your own fault, Tom Brown," she said. "You should not have attempted to follow me when I fled from here. 'Twas a most inglorious display you made at the best."

Tom hung his head.

" 'Twas dark, m'lady, and he was a terrible size of a man."

"Was he, Tom. How big was he?"

"Nigh seven feet tall, m'lady, and with shoulders like an ox. A giant he was—not a man, m'lady."

He looked about him carefully, then leaned over.

"Listen, m'lady, I don't believe he was a man at all."

She stared at him in amused surprise.

"Not a man, Tom, what was he then?"

"I think he was a spooky fellow, ma'am."

"A spooky fellow," she laughed. "What mean you?"

"A cloven hoof, m'lady, a livin' dead 'un. A horrid gobling."

She laughed now.

"What makes you think that, Tom?" she asked.

He looked at his feet and tried to appear very wise.

"I have my reasons, m'lady."

"Your reasons, Tom, and what are they?"

"Aye, well may you ask, m'lady," he muttered.

She stamped her little foot in temper now.

"Tell me at once, Tom Brown, what you mean. Do you hear?"

He looked about him again, then he said—

"Well, m'lady, 'tis like this. You see that night when we had the fight with this—this spooky giant, m'lady, I got to grips with him, and I happened to kinder notice that he wore a queer hat on his head. A tall hat it was, all covered with gray fur."

M'lady laughed.

"And so that frightened you, Tom."

He turned red and, forgetting himself, he spat upon the cobbles.

"Not that, m'lady, there is more than that."

"Well, go on, brave Tom."

"Well, ma'am, mebee you know that I'm a-courtin' Polly Marrow, the daughter o' the smith at Riverhead."

"Is that so, Tom? How very nice."

"Aye, m'lady, 'tis nice all right. Well, last night I was a-walking with Polly through the woods just off the highway near Riverhead, and we heard strange noises like some one panting hard near by. Well, I ain't no coward, m'lady, and I went forward into the wood a bit, and wot do you think I saw, m'lady?"

"I really can't guess, Tom. Please tell me."

Tom's voice was hoarse with excitement now.

"I saw a great figure loom up through the trees, ma'am, a gruesome, skeery figure, not like a man at all. And he was walking one way, and he had two heads, and one of the heads was looking over his back, and face of this head, ma'am, oh! the face."

Tom stopped and shuddered, while m'lady stared at him with wide eyes.

"Go on, go on," she gasped.

"It was something awful, ma'am. It was all mis-shaped, and it dangled loose like, and it was covered with blood, and the eyes stared like the eyes of a dead man."

"Well," said Lady Gloria.

"Well, m'lady, I was so skeered, I just stood rooted to the spot, but the gobling went right on into the woods."

"You're crazy, Tom," laughed Gloria, though a trifle shakily. "What has that to do with the man whom you fought?"

"Just this, m'lady," he said. "When the gobling had gone I went forward a bit into the woods and I stumbled over something, and I picked it up, and what do you think it was?"

"How should I know, Tom?" she answered impatiently.

He looked as impressive as possible.

"It was the tall, furry hat the man what helped you on the road wore."

There was dead silence for a few minutes, and then something made Gloria lift her gaze to the window where John Shale stood.

For a moment she stared full into his eyes. Then she turned swiftly, and walked away.

Suddenly, she stopped and turned back to Tom Brown again.

"What did you do with the hat you found, Tom?"

For answer, he walked into the washhouse and returned with the quaint old piece of headgear in his hand.

"Here 'tis, m'lady. Just as I found it."

She took it from him and, without a word, walked away with it.

And, while Tom looked after her and scratched his tousled head in perplexity, John Shale gave a deep sigh and, turning, walked back to the room where he had left Peter.

The latter was spreading out some more gorgeous garments of silk for wear at dinner that night.

"Peter," said Shale, looking down at his neat-trimmed finger nails.

"Yes, m'lord."

"Where were you last night?"

Peter bent and went on sorting the garments.

"I took a little walk last night, m'lord."

"Riverhead way?"

A silence, then——

"Aye, m'lord."

Another long silence.

"And what happened, Peter?"

Peter flushed, but he looked Shale full in the face.

"Well, m'lord, I—I carried him away to his —his last resting place, m'lord."

Shale bowed his head and swinging slowly round walked silently from the room.

And as he went, his mind visualized the scene which Tom Brown had undoubtedly witnessed —the stalwart Peter carrying the poor mutilated body of his dead master away from the pretty little glade in the woods.

SEES SHALE GIVING THREE MEN A NASTY SHOCK

SHALE went round to the stables.

He was curious to learn if Tom Brown's eyesight had been so good that night on the highway that he would recognize in his new master the adventurer who so successfully blackened his eye.

He found the stable boy still sitting on the upturned pail singing lustily.

> I love the beer
> That gives me cheer,
> When at the Inn I tarry me;
> But most of all
> I love sweet Poll,
> The maid that's going to marry me.

"Drat this eye of mine," he burst out suddenly.

"For why, Tom," put in Shale, arriving suddenly upon the scene.

The stable boy stared at him for a moment in amazement, then sprang to his feet and stood bowing awkwardly. 'Twas most unusual for his master to address him in tones other than curses.

"I asked why you should drat your eye, Tom," once more asked Shale, advancing and looking quizzically at him.

Tom spluttered for a few moments, then muttered:

"Because a maid I know hath sworn never to have aught to do with a fighting man, m'lord."

And again he tugged his forelock awkwardly.

"Is that sweet Poll the smith's daughter?" asked Shale.

Tom looked at him in amazement. Surely, m'lord did not know sweet Poll. Tom hoped he did not, right fervently, for he had heard enough of Lord Geoffrey Anderley to realize that his interest in a young village maid was something to be feared rather than to give pleasure.

"Aye, m'lord," he muttered, "but how did you guess."

Shale laughed.

"Never mind, Tom, but sing me another verse of your lovelorn song, and saddle me a good horse. I would ride me into Riverhead."

Tom blushed. He prided himself greatly upon his vocal capabilities, and it gave him real pleasure to think that m'lord appreciated them.

"Aye, aye, m'lord. Wilt have thy favorite the gray, or wilt have the roan?"

"Whichever you like," said Shale.   "It matters not to me."

Again Tom wondered, for as a rule Lord Anderley would never ride any but the great dapple-gray that had a better stride than any other beast throughout the countryside, and had never been known to be beaten in a race.

So taking no chances, Tom saddled the gray, and as he did so he sang at the pitch of his mellow voice.

> My Polly's eyes are like the skies,
>   Their color is the same;
> My Polly's hair is like the flare
>   That marks the leaping flame.
> Ah, you should see my Polly's feet,
> There's none in County Kent so neat,
> Nor is there e'en a maid so sweet,
>   And Polly is her name.
>
>   Oh, I love the hunt,
>   I love the hounds,
> I love my horse to carry me;
>   But most of all
>   I love sweet Poll,
> The maid that's going to marry me.
>
> Heigh-o, heigh-o! But I am a weary soul,
>   A-grooming horses all day long,
>   And singing of this lovesick song,
> That makes me feel more dole,
> Aye, that makes me feel more dole.

"Truly a weary song for such a merry wight as you, Tom," quoth Shale, mounting to the saddle and wheeling the great gray towards the stable gate. "But then you have a blackened eye, haven't you, Thomas?"

Tom muttered a curse.

"Aye, master, and I would I could meet the man that bestowed it on me, I'd mark him for life, m'lord."

Shale turned, amused.

"Faith, Tom, I wouldn't be too hard upon the knave. Perchance he is a harmless fellow who did not really mean to hurt you, and who could not help it that your head should get in the way of his fist."

"Aye, but he took me at a disadvantage, m'lord. If he'd been a real human, I'd have dumbed him."

"Dumbed him, Tom. What mean you, man?"

"Knocked him speechless, m'lord."

Shale laughed heartily.

"But was he not human, Tom?"

Tom looked about him.

"Nay, m'lord, 'e was a gobling, master, a great, gloomy gobling with arms like windmills and legs like church steeples, and his eyes were spurting fire, m'lord, and his hat——"

Here Shale laughed again, and spurred his horse.

"Aye, his hat, Tom. Was it not a tall furry hat, Tom?"

And as his hearty laughter echoed through the stable yard, Tom stood scratching his shock of hair in amaze.

"Now, and how did he know that," he muttered, as he turned once more to his cleaning and his singing.

Shale rode steadily through the great grounds towards the wide gate that opened on to the road to Riverhead.

As he rode, he failed to notice that he was being observed by a pair of sparkling eyes that gazed through a big mulberry bush, and, of course, he was not to know that Lady Gloria was actually giving vent to unwilling admiration of his fine seat and easy horsemanship.

The sun was shining warmly, and the birds were whistling merrily as Shale passed down the wooded road towards the village of Riverhead.

As he had expected, he was greeted as he entered the village with much bowing and scraping and tugging of forelocks on the part of the village folks, and the mothers ran to their doors with their little ones to point out Lord Anderley

to them, and to admire his fine clothes and handsome figure.

Swinging round into the main highway, Shale
approached the village inn—"The Amherst,"
which stands right upon the roadside, and hath
known some of the strangest adventures that
hath e'er taken place within four walls.

He tied his horse to a hitching post, and
mounted the little steps leading to the door of
the inn.

Pushing it open, he strode into the taproom
and ordered a mug of ale.

Shale had no particular desire to drink, but
the weather was warm and the roads were dusty
and, moreover, he considered a visit to the village inn a fine method of getting familiar with
the people, and perchance learning something
about the neighboring gentry.

He was also keenly anxious to learn if any
one other than Tom Brown and his sweetheart,
Poll, the smith's daughter, had seen Peter carrying the dead Lord Anderley from the glade the
previous night.

Three men were drinking at the bar when he
entered, and none of them looked round or observed him.

He walked a couple of paces into the room,
then stopped suddenly. One of the men was a

little fellow, plump and round, clad in long riding coat and longer jack boots. His companion was a tall, lanky fellow with cadaverous face, over which a long scar extended. The third man was evidently of high estate. His riding coat was richly decorated with gold lace, and he transported snuff in prodigious quantities from a large mull to his very big, bulbous nose.

He carried a riding whip, and a long sword was slung by his side. He was speaking to the landlord of the "Amherst," and his companions were listening intently to what he was saying.

"So you've had no word of mourning up at the hall, eh," he said.

The landlord shook his head.

"Nay, Sir Humphrey. Indeed I know well that you are mistaken, for Polly Marrow, the smith's daughter, hath a sweetheart in one of the grooms, and her father, Jem Marrow, the smith, tells me that m'lord hath returned from foreign parts."

"The devil he has," growled Sir Humphrey, looking hard at the men beside him, who fidgeted uneasily. "Faith, and somebody has been lying to me, and 'twill go ill with him an' I prove it."

A deep voice boomed out a hearty laugh.

" 'Tis easy to prove, Sir Humphrey, for here I am safe and sound, hale and hearty."

The three men wheeled round suddenly, and a hoarse cry broke from the tall, slim man's thin lips.

" 'Tis he," he cried.

Again Shale laughed, but this time it was not a laugh of mirth. Rather was it a harsh laugh that had a steely hardness in it, and sent a shiver down the backs of the three men.

"Aye, Simon Grappletight, 'tis I, and you seem none too glad to see me. Even little Benjamin Greenleaf who joked so merrily to me at the 'Whyte Hart' hath a queer look about him. Hey, Simon, you are going strangely white at the gills, man, and, zounds, little Ben is shaking so that he wobbles mightily. Dost know what you remind me of?"

Benjamin Greenleaf's eyes were well nigh starting from his head, as they stared fixedly and in terror at the face of Shale. He could not bring himself to answer, but merely shook the more violently.

"Zooks, man, where's your tongue? Dost know what you remind me of?"

Benjamin forced himself to shake his head, but kept staring terror-stricken at Shale.

Again the callous harsh laugh rasped out.

"You remind me of a hanged man I once saw swinging from a gibbet."

A dead silence followed. A silence which was broken at last by a convulsive sobbing gasp from Benjamin. It sounded almost like a sigh of relief, and now gradually the color came back into his cheeks. Simon emitted a long string of coarse curses and, turning, gulped down his ale so quickly, that he swallowed a vast quantity the wrong way, whereupon he spluttered the rest incontinently upon Sir Hurphrey's yellow waistcoat.

This made the latter swear most heartily, and for a full minute the rafters rang with a fine selection of oaths, while Shale stood by, a sardonic smile upon his lips.

And now Benjamin, having recovered his breath, bowed low.

" 'Tis good to see you, m'lord," he said. "Did'st have—have a pleasant journey from the 'Whyte-Hart' yon plaguy night?"

Shale looked at him long and steadily, a menacing gleam in his eye, that made the little fat man start to shiver again.

"Aye, pleasant enough," replied Shale, "and did you meet with any adventures."

"Nay," quoth Greenleaf, but here Sir Humphrey broke in.

"Ha, m'lord. So you're back again, eh? Well, here's health to you," and he raised his tankard.

Shale bowed stiffly. He had never met Sir Humphrey before, though he knew Anderley must have known him well.

"My health is good, Sir Humphrey," he replied in a suave voice, "and please God 'twill remain so."

Sir Humphrey took a sudden pinch of snuff, and drew it into his nose so heartily that he sneezed prodigiously several times.

"A tishoo!-Ha-a sneeze lads—a-a-a-atishoo-Gad! another sneeze—the first I've had for months, 'tis most welcome, most wel-a-a-a-atishoo-Grr!—by my periwig—a third, 'tis unheard of."

"Aye, but not unheard," laughed Shale, "but faith, my appearance seems to have caused much strange excitement."

"Excitement," gasped Sir Humphrey, "never was cooler in my life, save when I fought a duel with Sir Henry Golucky, and winged him too, egad."

This was the only time within knowledge that Sir Humphrey had crossed swords, and 'twas well known that Sir Henry was not only drunk at the time, but was also suffering from a bad attack of gout.

"But 'tis a warm day," added Shale.

"Aye, in truth, 'tis hot," agreed Sir Humphrey,

mopping his brow with a huge red kerchief.

"And yet you're very cool," went on Shale.

Sir Humphrey looked at him, and his face went purple.

"Don't scoff at me, m'lord," he roared. "Dost forget I once crossed swords with Sir Henry Golucky? Aye, and winged him too."

Shale laughed and shook his head.

"Faith, I've no wish to quarrel, Sir Humphrey," he said. "I was but curious as to whether you were hot or cool."

"I'm cool, man—d'ye hear—cool as a cucumber," and again he mopped his brow.

Shale drained his tankard.

"You mean you are cool, sir, but your head is hot."

"Hot be damned, sir. I'm cool—cool—cool, sir, and the devil take you.

Shale laughed.

"Then I may take it that you're cold, Sir 'Humph.' "

The knight went nigh black in the face.

"Cold, aye, cold, sir, if you like—but don't call me Sir—Sir—what you said, sir."

" 'Twas but a term of friendship, Sir Humph—Humph-rey. But it pleases me to know you're cool, for as our little friend Benjamin would say, being cool you are plainly cold, and being cold you are therefore cold blooded. Am I not right, Sir Humph—rey?"

The knight's face blanched a little before the steady, meaning stare of the other man, and the indignant string of curses which rose to his lips were choked back by a sudden deep draught of ale.

He strove to speak naturally, as if he were not laboring under the stress of any untoward excitement.

"And—and what are you to do at the hall, Anderley," he said. "Your aunt has my niece, Gloria, there, but belike 'tis too dull for you after Paris, eh!"

Shale shook his head.

" 'Tis a relief to get back amongst honest folks," he said, "and now, dear friends, I must away. My Lady Gloria is a beauteous maid, Sir Humphrey. 'Tis strange, is it not, that she should be your niece?"

Sir Humphrey gasped, choked and spluttered, but ere he recovered his breath, Shale moved to the door with an airy wave of his hand, such as would have done justice to any French courtier.

"Adieu," he called.

"Farewell," growled Simon, the only one who had kept his senses.

Shale paused.

"Nay, Simon, as I said that night at the 'Whyte Hart,' *au-revoir,* mayhap we will meet again."

There was dead silence while Simon glared and Benjamin shuffled uneasily.

Then Shale spoke again.

"Why now say 'mayhap, we will, master,' Simon," he urged. " 'Twould make the memory complete."

But Simon only glared the fiercer, and with a light taunting laugh, Shale stepped from the inn, and swung into the saddle of his great gray horse.

INTRODUCES A RIVAL WHO ALSO FENCES

S HALE rode quietly through the little village
of Riverhead searching for the smithy.

He had just reached the end of the village,
and was thinking he must have missed it by some
chance when there rose upon the warm midday
air the cheery ring of hammer upon anvil, and
the deep tones of a lusty voice keeping time with
each blow after this fashion:

> Good steel, true steel,
> When you turn blue steel;
> Blow, bellows, blow,
> Till the metal glow.
> Smite, man, smite,
> Till the glow is white,
> And the smithy's full of starry sparks,
> Like summer skies at night,
> Like summer skies at night.

Thus Shale knew that he was come to the
smithy, and advancing under an archway he saw
at the other end of the yard Jem Marrow, the
smith, himself.

123

He was a stalwart figure, a big man even for a smith, and with each mighty blow of his heavy hammer the sparks sprang out in all directions from the horseshoe he was making.

His hair was white, but long and thick and curly. He looked a picturesque figure standing there with the sweat from his brow trickling down his rugged clean-shaven features.

And ever and anon he dashed it away with a motion of the back of his great hairy arm across his forehead.

His rough shirt was open wide at the neck, and a leather apron hung about his waist.

Near by stood a typical gallant from London, and Shale noted at once that it was this man's horse that the smith was shoeing. He was a fairly tall fellow, elaborately dressed, even more elaborately than Shale himself, and his periwig was powdered lavishly. He reeked of perfume from the shoulder straps of his silk-lined riding coat to the tops of his glossy polished boots. His spurs were of gold, and his heels were painted to match.

His face had once been handsome, and even yet he was good to look upon, but fast living and deep dissipation had left their mark upon him. There was a sallow puffiness under the eyes, a haggard, blotchy look about the face that spoke of countless nights of revelry and indulgence in excesses of every description.

He looked what he was—a typical roué of the day—a deep drinker, a shameless profligate, and he looked no less such because his countenance contrasted so deeply with that of the buxom girl who stood blushing prettily before him.

Shale guessed at once that she was Polly Marrow, the smith's daughter.

"An' you'll give me but one taste of your sweet lips," said the gallant, slipping his arm around the girl's waist.

The ringing of hammer upon steel stopped suddenly, and the smith looked round at the couple.

None seemed to have observed Shale's entrance, leading his horse by the bridle.

"Nay, sir," said Polly, blushing deeper. "I cannot an' it please you, sire. I am betrothed."

"Ha, ha!" quoth the gallant, "so much the better. Your innocence will have the added charm of experience. Come! just one."

Something like a growl came from the smith, and he stood up straight, his shoulders heaving mightily.

"Poll," he said sharply, "get about the house duties, 'tis nigh time my midday meal were prepared."

With an artful wriggle, buxom Polly escaped from the grasp of her unwelcome admirer, and ran laughing into the house while her father smiled grimly at the courtier's chagrin.

The latter emitted an elaborate oath, one fashionable at the Court at that time, and turning caught sight of Shale.

Instantly his brows contracted slightly and something like viciousness flashed into his dark eyes. Then with an obvious effort at camaraderie he burst out:

"Why, plague me, if it isn't Anderley. Gad, man, and 'tis long since I saw you."

Shale bowed, but being at a distinct disadvantage by not knowing who the man was decided to await developments. As he expected, the other quickly revealed his identity.

"What, Anderley," he cried, seeing the blank look upon the other's handsome face. "Don't ye know me, man. Don't you know Aylesbury, sir. Why, demme, sir, the last time we met there were a pair o' blades betwixt us, and I spit you through the left leg. Now, you remember me, egad!"

So this was Aylesbury, Sir Claude Aylesbury, reputed to be the finest swordsman England had known. And he had evidently had a duel with Anderley at some time or other, and had come

off best, despite m'lord's fine fencing. Shale
knew him well by name, for he had large estates
Otford way, and many stories circulated throughout the countryside as to his wild doings, and
the great drinking and gambling parties that took
place at his manor.

Shale recollected that his father had told him
that he had once crossed swords with the roué,
and that he was a magnificent fighter. "We
fought for a full hour," the elder Shale had said,
"and neither of us drew a drop of blood. In
the end we lowered blades and shook hands."

He must have been a very young man then,
thought John as he viewed the graceful figure
and sallow face of the other. Now he must be a
man in the late forties, but probably was more
skillful and cunning with the sword than ever.

Shale bowed low.

"Faith, I remember you well, Aylesbury," he
replied, tendering him his snuff box, "and I
have good cause to remember you too."

Aylesbury laughed, but there was something
like a sneer in his voice.

"Gad! it comes to every man to be beaten,"
he said, "but, faith, I have to meet my master
yet."

"I doubt you never will," murmured Shale.

" 'Tis demnably pleasant to think so. And

it must be demnably unpleasant to meet your better, too, eh, Anderley."

Shale laughed with a hard ring in his mirth.

"Demnably, as you say."

"When did you get back from France?" queried Aylesbury.

"But two days gone."

"And didst leave all in Paris well. What's the latest gossip there?"

"Nay, Aylesbury, ask me not, for I've done little else but retail it since my return, and I never was a lover o' gossip."

This made Aylesbury roar.

"Ha, ha, ha, that's good, demned good. And 'twas the unfolding of a piece of gossip which linked your name with a wench I had a notion of that we fell out over."

Shale frowned. Was he never to escape being blamed for the wretched love affairs of the real Anderley.

"You mean?" he queried.

"Mean," scoffed Aylesbury, "aye, you know well who I mean. Who other but the Lady Gloria Clayville who has us both kicking our heels in these demned parts awaiting her every precious little whim."

Shale's frown deepened.

So for once Lord Geoffrey Anderley had

fought in a just cause. 'Twas a pity he had not fought better though, and laid this braggart low.

" 'Twould have saved me the work o' doing it," muttered Shale.

"What say you?" asked Aylesbury sharply. Shale sighed.

"I say that 'twill lie with m'lady to decide, sir." The other laughed coarsely.

"Aye, in part it will, but much of it will lie with you or me, man, and as far as I'm concerned, I'll leave no stone unturned to bring her tidy little fortune into my own pocket."

Shale felt he could have run the man through then and there, and it was with difficulty that he restrained himself from making some challenging remark.

Instead, however, he turned, and looking over Aylesbury's horse which was just finished shoeing and champed impatiently, he adroitly turned the subject by commenting on its points.

Aylesbury tossed the smith a piece of silver, and the latter led the horse out through the arch under an overhanging building to the highway, where he held it for Aylesbury to mount.

"Art journeying just now, Anderley," he asked as he gathered up his reins, "or are you to have your horse shod, too."

"I tarry but for a word with the smith, friend," replied Shale.

Aylesbury guffawed once more, then spurred his horse.

"I'll wager me 'tis over his pretty daughter," he called. "Gad! Anderley, can you not let alone the village wenches, even when you're a-wooin' a lady fair?"

Shale ground his teeth, and glared viciously after the departing knight, but next moment he had recovered himself, and was smiling amiably to the big smith.

The latter eyed him with obvious surprise. Even though M'lord Anderley was his landlord, and had ever been a tolerably lenient one, big Jem Marrow knew enough of lords and their codes of honor to view any display of apparent friendship with distrust.

"Well, m'lord," he growled, tugging at a lock of his white hair, more out of diplomacy than servility. "What would you ask of me?"

"It concerns your daughter, Polly," quoth m'lord.

Jem Marrow's brow contracted, and his jaw went forward.

"Well," he growled.

Shale smiled.

" 'Tis but a small matter, smith. Is she not

betrothed to one of my stablemen, a fellow named Tom Brown?"

"Aye, m'lord," still distrustfully.

"Well," said Shale, "Tom was out with her last night awalking in the woods near here, and he declares that he saw a hideous goblin. I was amused, and, passing, thought I would hear what Polly said of it."

A sigh of relief escaped Jem Marrow, and without a word he walked into his house and shouted to Polly to come out.

"Tell m'lord what ye saw last night, girl," he ordered when the pretty little wench appeared blushing before m'lord.

"In the woods, mean you?" she asked demurely.

"Aye, lady," quoth Shale, whereupon Polly blushed more furiously at the great compliment the unexpected term conveyed, but forthwith began to outline the experience of the night before.

" 'Twas Tom saw it first, m'lord," she said, "and he pointed at it without speaking not so much as a word. Then I looked, m'lord, and I saw the most fearsomest gobling as ever was. At first, it looked like a gobling, m'lord, but it looked like as if some one was carrying a dead man, too."

"Eh!" ejaculated Shale sharply. "You seem a shrewd little maid."

She curtsied sweetly.

"Hast told a soul in the village of this?" Shale demanded.

She shook her head.

"I was greatly a-feared, m'lord. None but Tom and my father know of it."

Shale nodded, and taking out his purse, presented Polly with a golden guinea.

"Well, see that the tale goes no further," he commanded, "and perchance there will be a cottage to spare when you and Tom want to wed. I am curious to know what is behind the tale, and want none to become aware of it, and push their meddlesome noses into what concerns them nought."

And followed by the bewildered thanks of the delighted girl, Shale passed out of the yard.

The smith held his horse for him, and after he was in the saddle, stood back tugging his white locks again, but this time with real reverence.

"God speed you, m'lord," he growled, and his deep voice quivered a trifle. "An' you save that cottage for my lass and her man, you'll ne'er want for a friend as long as Jem Marrow, the smith, has life."

"Thank you, Jem," said Shale, and then with a pretty wave of his hand to wonderstruck Polly he turned his horse in the direction of Bessels Green.

The Smith watched him till he turned the corner at the cross roads and passed from view, then he went back to his anvil.

And as the sparks flew and the happy jingle of his hammer rang out once more, he lifted his deep voice and sang merrily:

> Good steel, true steel,
> When you turn blue steel;
> Blow, bellows, blow,
> Till the metal glow.
> Smite, man, smite,
> Till the glow is white,
> And the smithy's full of starry sparks,
> Like summer skies at night,
> Like summer skies at night.

FINDS LADY GLORIA INTERESTED

SHALE was met at the gates of Anderley Hall by Peter mounted on a chestnut pony.

He was galloping down the wide drive when his master caught sight of him, and he was urging his horse to further effort with spur and whip, an unusual thing for him to do, for he was generally most considerate of his mount.

"Master! master!" he called, as he drew up alongside Shale. "'Tis glad in truth I am to see you back again."

"For why, Peter, what's amiss?"

"Zookers, 'tis nothing mighty serious, m'lord, only—Sir Humphrey Clayville is here."

Shale laughed.

"Well, there's naught strange in that, Peter, since I met him myself in the 'Amherst.' What makes you so excited, man?"

"Well, m'lord, an' I guess a-right he is here to take M'lady Gloria back to Clayville Grange."

Again Shale laughed, though this time a trifle hardly.

134

"Well, who has a better right, Peter? Is he not her uncle and guardian?"

"Aye, m'lord, but he bodes her no good. Consider, m'lord, he hath one death on his hands to account for already."

Shale drew up his horse suddenly and swore.

"Gad, man, you don't mean he'd harm m'lady?"

Peter shook his head doubtfully.

"Perhaps not, m'lord, but failing other means of getting the gold to himself, I'd put nothing beyond him."

Shale rode on frowning till they reached the steps leading to the big door of the hall.

A stableboy stood outside holding a big black horse. It was Sir Humphrey Clayville's, and Shale remembered having seen it tethered in the yard at the "Amherst."

He dismounted and, as Peter led away his horse, he leapt up the steps and passed into the great paneled hall.

For a moment he paused, undecided, then the sound of voices coming from the cool, shady lounge on the left, smote his listening ears.

Without tarrying further, he strode towards the room and entered.

On the threshold he paused, and surveyed the group before him. It consisted of the Lady Gloria, his aunt and Sir Humphrey Clayville.

The latter's florid face was redder even than usual, and 'twas plain he was in a temper, a by no means unusual thing with him, as his servants knew to their cost. He was speaking loud and forcibly, punctuating his remarks with pushes upon the hilt of his sword, which caused the scabbard to rise suddenly, throwing the tails of his riding coat in the air.

"I tell you, Lady Genevieve Collingway (her full title), that Gloria is coming back with me to the Grange. I've put up enough with your scheming for her to make a match of it with Anderley, and 'tis time she was back at her own home again. I only permitted her to come here because I knew Anderley was in Paris. Now that he is back, 'tis for her to return. Besides, I have need of her to act as hostess at a reception to-morrow night."

"And I tell you, Sir Humphrey," broke in Lady Genevieve, in her calm, but very determined little voice, "that Gloria is staying here for a few days more. You know as well as I do that it is essential that she and Geoffrey should meet. Her father has decreed it, and I am going to see that his wishes are carried out, for I love her too well to let her estates pass into your gentle keeping."

"Grrr-grr-grr," snarled Sir Humphrey, like a

dog at bay. Being afraid to swear in the presence of Lady Genevieve, he could perforce do nothing else than snarl, but he certainly did snarl well and with extreme thoroughness.

But now Lady Gloria broke in with merry voice.

"And while you two are squabbling there about me, Lord Anderley himself watches you with unconcealed amusement."

All turned and stared at Shale standing at the door with a soft smile upon his lips. He bowed deeply.

"Faith, 'tis a lovely day to spend indoors in this fashion, dear folks," he said, his deep voice booming through the heavy curtained room. "And, prithee, why this strange excitement?"

Lady Gloria dropped a pretty curtsey. She was dressed in a sweet silken dress all covered with summer flowers in beauteous hues, with a little sun hat upon her head, and its ribbons knotted 'neath her dimpled chin.

Shale felt his breath draw in sharply as he looked upon her loveliness.

"The cause of all the babble, sir, is me—poor little me"—she said with a merry laugh that sounded to Shale like the tinkling of silver bells. "Your aunt wants me to stay here, and my uncle desires me to depart. Wilt play arbiter?"

Shale shook his head with a smile.

"Nay, 'twere too grave a responsibility, rather would I suggest that the matter be left for settlement with your sweet self."

Again that tinkling laugh.

" 'Tis a sound suggestion, but one that will not appeal to your aunt, who hath already kept me here by sheer force, and will not scruple to employ it once again."

"I think not, m'lady," quoth Shale, " 'tis plain that you desire to depart and since to me your merest wish is law, then depart you shall, though 'twill go hard with all of us to lose you."

"Geoffrey!" broke in Aunt Genevieve in consternation, "think what you do"—but Lady Gloria stayed her.

Her eyes were flashing a little. Whate'er the wish of any maid might be, 'twas something in the nature of a snub to be told that whenever she wished to depart she could do so.

A moment before she had been determined and eager to leave Anderley Hall, but now she did not view the prospect with any of the pleasure she had anticipated.

"Do be quiet, Aunt Genevieve," she said, for though she was no relation, she always referred to Lady Collingway as Aunt Genevieve. "If

M'lord Anderley is eager for me to depart, 'tis indeed a pleasure for me to give him his wish."

Shale looked full at her while Sir Humphrey grinned, and rubbed his fat hands with satisfaction.

"Dear m'lady," said the new Lord Anderley, "you purposely misjudge my words. I but anticipated your own fervent desire. If so be it you would rather stay here a space, well 'tis I will most appreciate your condescension."

Lady Gloria laughed again, a shade more merrily this time.

"Faith, our lord makes pretty speeches. Uncle, we'll need to send you to Paris for a spell, methinks."

Sir Humphrey growled, but, heeding him not, Lady Gloria proceeded.

"However, m'lord, since 'tis left to me to decide, I will depart. But lest you think 'twere discourteous of me to leave you thus, I will grant you the pleasure of meeting me again at the reception at the Grange to-morrow evening. What say you, Uncle?"

Sir Humphrey frowned and stamped, then with ill grace asked Shale to accept the invitation which he forced himself to say he "had come specially to the Hall to tender."

Shale bowed.

"I shall be there, m'lady, amongst the earliest guests, and I trust you may be disposed to walk with me a minuet?"

"As we do it in London," she cried, gaily dropping a curtsey. "But not in your most approved Parisian style."

Shale laughed a little awkwardly.

"Faith, 'tis little I know of either," he replied.

"Ah, then," quoth Sir Humphrey, with sudden interest, "you'll spend thy time with us less sprightly fellows at the card tables."

He slapped his thigh and again cautioned Shale to be sure to come, and this time he spoke with genuine persuasion.

And Lady Gloria, knowing her uncle well, frowned and pondered on the matter in her pretty little head.

The Lady Genevieve protested strongly against Gloria's departure, but Shale only smiled, and the little minx laughed and gave orders for her pony to be saddled while she departed to don her riding habit.

Half an hour later, Shale assisted Lady Gloria into her saddle, and stood for a moment looking up at her.

"Ah, m'lady," he said softly, "the hours will drag until the morrow."

She looked at him with a little frown.

"I wonder how many ladies in Paris you have said that to, Lord Anderley," she replied.

He drew back.

"M'lady, an' you believe me, none."

She drew a quick little breath and laughed.

"Faith, then, some tales must be sadly exaggerated."

He bowed.

"Aye, 'tis a habit tales have," he said. "I heard a tale but two nights since concerning one I hold in high esteem, and I doubted not 'twas most grossly exaggerated."

She looked down at him with sudden interest.

"And what did you do, m'lord?"

He smiled.

"Faith, I could but listen, though later I had the pleasure of teaching the man who told the tale a lesson—poor fellow."

She flushed slightly, for no reason that she could think of.

"Ah, whom did that tale concern, m'lord?"

He turned slowly away without answering, and now he observed that Peter was standing by his side, having just assisted Sir Humphrey's corpulent carcass on to the back of his black horse.

"Wilt not tell me, m'lord?" once more asked

Lady Gloria, and she seemed very eager for an answer.

"Come along," called Sir Humphrey, waving his hat in adieu to Lady Genevieve.

Shale stood impassive, his broad shoulders squared, his firm chin forward, a slight smile upon his handsome face.

Lady Gloria frowned, and touched her horse with her riding crop.

As she did so, Peter stepped forward.

"M'lady, the tale m'lord spoke of concerned——"

"Who, Peter?" she demanded quickly.

"You—m'lady—you."

She looked far away over the tree tops, then: "Peter."

"Yes, m'lady."

"To-morrow morning you will ride over to the Grange. I would speak with you."

Peter beamed.

"Aye, m'lady, and thank you."

But now her crop flicked the mare's flank again, and it sprang lightly forward.

At the first bend in the drive she turned in her saddle and looked for a brief moment at Shale standing bareheaded watching her. Then she was gone.

Shale turned to Peter.

"Peter," he said.

"Aye, m'lord."

"You're a fool, Peter."

"Aye, m'lord."

Shale looked fixedly at him, then turned away with a sigh.

"But not such a fool as I am, Peter."

"Zookers, m'lord. And for why, m'lord?"

"For why, Peter. For thinking I am what I am not, Peter, and also for being what I am."

And as he walked slowly down the rose-covered avenue to the beautiful bower at its end, Peter ejaculated once more:

"Zookers!"

But m'lord heard him not.

He was looking down softly at the little seat where first he had seen her.

"And she was weeping," he murmured, "weeping for me. Because she believes that I am what he was. And yet I would that I were, for then might I with easy heart and mind lay my love at her little feet to spurn or cherish as she please."

And he sat slowly down, and hid his face in his hands; while Peter watched him from afar with a queer unaccountable moisture in his eyes.

WHERE PETER PUTS IN A WORD FOR HIS MASTER

THE Lady Gloria was balanced upon a chair which stood on the top of the great table in the banqueting hall of Clayville Grange.

She was busily engaged stringing garlands of roses from one great candelabra to the other, and she was doing it exceedingly well. Her nimble little fingers twined the roses in and out with amazing dexterity, and blended their colors with wonderful artistry.

Sir Humphrey Clayville, stamping into the room, making it shake with the noise of his heavy riding boots upon the oaken floor, stopped short near the door when he saw his niece at work.

"Gad," he grunted, his big rough voice drowning the dying jingle of his spurs. "You're busy, Gloria. Can't understand what induces you to meddle about with housework when there are dozens of servants kept for it."

"Please to mind your own business, Sir Humphrey Clayville," retorted m'lady. "Remember I shall do as I please in my own house."

A nasty gleam came into Sir Humphrey's eyes. He hated to be reminded that Clayville Grange belonged to Lady Gloria, and not to him.

"Demme, Gloria, and what do you think my business is if it's not to look after you?"

She tilted her little nose into the air, and shook her golden curls.

"Look after me, indeed, Uncle Humphrey. Faith, you've more need to look after yourself. I heard you falling downstairs last night when you were trying to go up, and I notice that your nose is redder than usual this morning. I'm sure you might have been more careful, seeing all the nobility from London gather here to-night to open our house party. 'Tis certain your nose will be red enough 'ere 'tis finished."

Sir Humphrey forgot that he was in the presence of a lady, and swore loud and deep.

Gloria plugged her ears with her fingers.

"For shame, Sir Humphrey Clayville. You must think you are in the taproom of the 'Amherst' or the 'Golden Pig.'"

"Gadzooks and zounds, Gloria, your tongue should be tied up with hempen rope," he roared.

She looked at him tantalizingly.

"What makes you think of a hempen rope, Uncle, dear. It always suggests the hangman and gibbets, and gruesome things like that to me."

The oaths froze on Sir Humphrey's thick lips, and the color slowly faded from his cheeks. He swayed as he stood, and there was a terror-stricken look in his eyes.

Gloria stared at him in amazement.

"Why, what's the matter, Uncle Humphrey?" she asked, getting quickly down from her chair and running over to him. "Do you feel ill?"

He passed his hand across his head and, crossing over to the serving table, poured himself out a stiff glass of brandy, which he swallowed at a gulp.

Then as the color came gradually back to his fat cheeks again, he laughed jerkily.

"A sudden faintness, Gloria, that's all," he muttered. "Too much to drink last night. I'll go out and have a breath of air, it will revive me somewhat."

He stamped fiercely from the room, while Gloria gazed at his retreating form in wonderment.

"Now I wonder what made him turn white like that," she said to herself. " 'Tis a thing I never knew Uncle Humphrey do before. What was it I said, now; let me think. Oh, yes, something about a hempen rope and—and—hangman and gibbets—oo—oo, it is gruesome. But—but why should it make him go white? 'Tis strange, 'tis strange."

She went slowly back to her work, and was just climbing on to the table again when a footman, clad in elaborate livery, entered and announced:

"Master Peter Cherryblossom, from Anderley Hall, is here, m'lady. He says you told him to call."

Gloria jumped down to the floor again.

"Yes, James, show him in here, please, at once."

The man gave a stiff bow and departed. A minute later there was a sound of a deep voice in the hall.

"Well, I told you she wanted to see me, didn't I? Zookers, man, but you'd have done well to save yourself the journey to ask her. You'll wear out these spindle shanks of yours if you're not careful."

Gloria giggled, but controlled her features as Peter, clad in his best clothes, entered and stood pulling his forelock at the door.

"Morning, m'lady."

"Good morning, Peter."

Peter turned and looked severely at James, the footman.

"You may go, James," said Lady Gloria sweetly, and Peter grinned broadly.

"I wish you wouldn't tease James so, Peter," said Gloria, "it quite upsets him."

"Now that's a pity, m'lady, 'cos if he worries any more he'll be off his pins, m'lady, zookers, he will."

"Peter," said Gloria, severely. "How often have I told you not to say zookers to me? How often?"

Peter shook his head.

"I don't know, m'lady. About a thousand times by zookers—er, I'm sorry, m'lady, but I just can't help it. It comes sorter by itself."

"I see, it's a habit."

"Well, m'lady, 'taint quite a habit 'cos a habit has to be acquired. But zookers, ma'am, zookers to me is more in the nature of a—a—a—gift, ma'am."

Gloria laughed unrestrainedly.

"Peter, you're verily incorrigible, but 'tis not to teach you pretty sayings or to unlearn you silly ones that I asked you to call."

She turned to the table.

"As a matter of fact, Peter, I remembered yesterday how helpful you were when we celebrated Aunt Genevieve's birthday, long, long ago at the

Hall, and how you assisted me to do the decorations."

Peter's face fell visibly.

He remembered well that day, and how he had been chaffed mercilessly by the kitchen hands afterwards and most of all by Lady Genevieve, who insisted upon him decorating the rose bowls every day for weeks afterwards. He groaned.

"Well, m'lady, 'tis a pleasure to assist, but—but—m'lady."

"Well, Peter," she asked in surprise. "Of course, if you'd rather not——"

"Nay, nay, m'lady," hastily added Peter, " 'twas but a modest request I'd make."

"Go on, Peter."

"Well, ma'am," he said desperately, "please will you not tell any one at the Hall, and please may I shut the door so that James, the footman, can't see me."

She laughed merrily.

"All right, Peter, close the door an' you will."

With a sigh of relief, Peter pushed to the door, and put a chair against it. Then taking off his coat he rolled up his sleeves, and scrambled up on the table.

"You tell me where to hang 'em, ma'am, an' I'll stick 'em up."

In a few minutes he was busily engaged tying

the streamers of flowers across the candelabra.

"And how was it m'lord came to fight a duel on my account?" demurely asked Gloria after a while.

Peter started so violently he nearly fell off the chair.

"What's the matter, Peter?" cried Gloria, jumping back for fear he would come crashing down upon her.

He steadied himself.

"Zookers, m'lady, but that was a near thing," he muttered.

They went on working for a space.

"Well," she said again, "you haven't answered me yet, Peter."

He was prepared for her this time, and not even a zookers escaped his lips. He fixed a rose daintily in place, surveyed the effect, and then deigned to answer.

"You asked how m'lord came to fight a duel on your account, m'lady. Faith, he's fought two that I know of."

She pondered.

"H'm, one was with Sir Claude Aylesbury, two years ago, wasn't it?"

"Aye, m'lady."

"Yes, I heard of that," she said dryly. "That

was not a very glorious display. He was badly wounded, wasn't he."

"Yes, m'lady," agreed Peter, "but Sir Claude is the finest swordsman in England, ma'am, at least he was, m'lady."

"What do you mean by he was, Peter?"

"Nothing, m'lady. Just that maybe there's a better by this time."

"Well, there's not," she snapped. "I don't like him, but he's a wonderful fencer, and easily the best I've seen. I believe he just played with Lord Anderley."

Peter worked on in silence.

"But what was the duel, three nights ago, about, Peter?"

"Well, m'lady, I don't just know if I ought to tell you, but it happened at the 'Whyte Hart,' just beyond Sevenoaks, ma'am."

Gloria's thoughts flew back to that night in the dark roadway when a man with a tall furry hat had fought by her side. It must have been to the 'Whyte Hart' he meant her to try to run to that night. And all the while she was trying to escape, the man she was fleeing from was fighting for her.

"Yes, go on, Peter. How did the trouble start?"

"Well, ma'am, there was some one—ahem—

yes some one there who told a story about you, m'lady, which didn't please—him."

"Who, Peter?"

"The master, ma'am."

"What was the story?"

"I—I wouldn't just like——"

"Go on, Peter, tell me."

Peter took a deep breath.

"Well, ma'am, it was something to the effect that you fought a duel with an aged gallant, m'lady, and if you lost you was to marry him."

She frowned.

"Yes, I've heard the tale, Peter. But there's absolutely no truth in it."

"I knew it, m'lady," hastily added Peter.

"And did they fight over that?"

"Well, pretty much that, m'lady. You see this—this other fellow he wanted to drink a toast to Lady Gloria, the girl who'd—who'd——"

"Go on, Peter," said the firm little voice.

"To the girl who was willing to wed any man who could outmatch her in swordplay, m'lady."

"I—I see," said Gloria. "And I suppose M'lord Anderley resented that since—since common talk hath coupled our names together."

"The—the master resented it, m'lady."

She smiled.

"I'm quite glad, Peter. I like to think your master is a real man."

"He is, ma'am," said Peter fervently. "He's the finest man I've ever met."

Gloria smiled at his devotion, then:

"Who was the other man, Peter?"

Again Peter started so violently he nearly capsized. She looked at him curiously.

"Zookers, ma'am, I forgot his name."

She frowned.

"How was he dressed?"

Peter breathed a sigh of relief. As she had not seen Shale (so he thought) till he came to the Hall when he wore Anderley's coat and hat, he felt that he was quite safe to give a meager description of him.

"I don't rightly remember, ma'am, but I do know that he wore a tall furry hat."

This time m'lady started, and almost at once Peter realized that he had said too much.

She recovered herself almost immediately.

"Are you sure it was a tall furry hat, Peter?"

He scratched his head thoughtfully.

"Well, I'm not quite certain, ma'am. You see there were one or two other men at the inn, ma'am, and I may have got them mixed up."

"But you're certain that Lord Anderley didn't wear one," she put in.

Again he scratched his head.

"Zookers, m'lady, I'm danged if I can remember."

She sniffed indignantly.

"Peter," she said, handing him a long garland of roses, "you're lying to me."

He looked confused, and felt decidedly uncomfortable. He had come to the Grange determined to help in his master's cause, but instead he seemed to be ruining it completely.

"What was the other man, Peter—a courtier or a commoner. I suppose he was a courtier?"

"No, ma'am. At least he was quite a gentleman, ma'am, but he—he was dressed like a farmer, ma'am."

Another long silence.

"I hope Lord Anderley didn't kill him."

Peter looked at her in amaze.

"Kill him, ma'am. No fear—why——"

He broke off suddenly, but again he was too late.

"Go on, Peter," said that insistent little voice.

Peter coughed awkwardly.

"Well," she asked.

"Who won the fight, Peter?"

A long silence.

"I suppose the farmer won it, Peter."

Peter gulped and nodded his head.

She laughed queerly.

"Oh, you poor simple Peter. Of course, the farmer won, and yet he did not wound Lord Anderley."

"No, ma'am, he—he played a wonderful trick on him, and then let him off."

There was a long silence during which they went on working busily.

And now the garlands were all hung, and Peter dismounted from the table, and they stood back surveying their handiwork.

"Your master is coming to-night, isn't he?" she said disinterestedly.

"Yes, ma'am, so I believe, m'lady."

She crossed to the table which was still strewn with roses, and selecting two tiny pure white buds she tied them together with a little leafy spray behind them and handed them to Peter. And there was something like tears in her eyes as she spoke.

"Will you please give this little bouquet—to—to your master, Peter, and ask him to accept it from—from the Lady Gloria?"

Then blushing prettily she ran through the wide open French window out into the garden, and was lost to sight—a rose amongst other roses, while Peter stood staring stupidly at the little buds in his great clumsy paw.

"Zookers," he burst out suddenly, scratching his red head in perplexity. "Zookers! and like-wise ziggers!"

SOME STUTTERING AND THE APPOINTMENT OF
SECONDS

"HA-HA-HA—demmed good—demmed good,
he-he-he!"

Sir Claude Aylesbury threw back his head till
his flushed face pointed towards the ceiling of
the banqueting hall, as he gave vent to his burst
of laughter.

He sat on one side of the Lady Gloria. John
Shale sat on the other.

Sir Claude's mirth, loud and boisterous, as a
result of copious draughts of wine he had im-
bibed, was the outcome of a coarsely witty
remark by Sir Humphrey Clayville.

Sir Claude was the only one of that great and
gallant company who laughed. Several of the
young bloods smiled broadly, but M'lady Gloria
only frowned. It did not please her to hear her
uncle refer as a joke to his taproom jovialities.

"Ho-ho-ho," roared Sir Claude, shaking like
the red jelly shape on his plate. "Ho-ho-ah-ah-
hem-ahem."

He had suddenly caught sight of the frown on

157

Gloria's face, and his unseemly mirth subsided as suddenly as it had arisen.

"Zounds, m'lady," he said, mopping his brow with a great crimson silk kerchief. "Why that freezy stare? I'faith, I was enjoying the joke most hugely when the iciness o' thy countenance froze me mirth."

Gloria tossed her head disdainfully.

" 'Tis not o' the best taste to tell coarse jests in a lady's company, Sir Claude," she said, "and 'tis no less unmannerly to laugh at them."

Sir Claude went purple, and gulped down a mouthful of wine so hurriedly that he spluttered and then sneezed, making the whole company smile most genuinely.

Gloria turned to Shale, to whom she had hardly spoken till now.

"And what think you of our English dinners after your long experience of the French?" she asked in quite a friendly voice.

Shale, who had been dividing his attention between a stout dame on his right, who insisted upon heaping his plate with toothsome delicacies, despite his protestations, and an equally stout gentleman opposite, who was the dame's spouse, and who pushed his own plate forward every time John got another helping, was glad of her questioning.

"I'faith, m'lady," quoth Shale. "You do things most splendidly, and even the royal banquets in Paris could not compare with these wonderful dishes."

She smiled prettily.

"Quite an accomplished flatterer, m'lord. Another Parisian art, methinks."

Shale shook his head, smiling.

"Nay, m'lady, I give you my word, I flatter not. In solemn truth I do declare I never sat before at so kingly a table and," here his voice dropped low, "if so I may say, m'lady, ne'er have I met so queenly a hostess."

The soft color dyed her pretty cheeks.

"Ah," she murmured. " 'Tis as I said—brave flatterer."

He looked at her, and shook his head slowly.

" 'Tis useless for me to make denial, m'lady, but you know it well I mean my words."

She turned away to hide her face from him, lest he should see the blushes.

Suddenly she looked up at the garlands of roses twined amidst the brilliantly illuminated candelabra. The murmur of jovial conversation filled the room, intermingled with little bursts of laughter, the clink of glasses, and the clatter of spoons on plates.

"Your flattery is so pretty, despite that it is

but flattery, that I needs must seek for more of it," she said. "Did'st notice the flowers amidst the candelabra?"

"Aye, m'lady, I noticed them the instant that I entered me this room."

She laughed gaily.

"And why did you observe them so promptly?" she asked.

He thrust his hand into the pocket of his silken coat and withdrew a lily-white kerchief wrapped into a ball.

"Dost see this, m'lady?" he asked.

She looked at the trifle in surprise.

"Most surely I do, m'lord; but what has that to do with the roses in the candelabra?"

For answer he folded back the corners of the handkerchief and revealed, nestling softly in its silken bed, a tiny little bouquet consisting of two rosebuds and a green leaf.

Again the deep color suffused Gloria's cheeks, and again she had perforce to hide her face from Shale. But 'twas quite unnecessary, for he was not looking at her. He was gazing down tenderly at the flowers.

Then slowly he folded them up in the kerchief again, and replaced them carefully in his pocket.

" 'Twas you who made these decorations, m'lady, was it not?" he asked.

She laughed merrily, though withal a little shakily. Why should she feel so strangely affected by these little courtesies of this man? No doubt they were cunningly contrived and well practiced.

"Forsooth, m'lord, you are wondrous good at guessing; well nigh as good as you are at flattery. 'Tis plain you must have had equal practice."

Shale looked at her steadily, then, after a long time, he sighed deeply and took a little sip from his red wine.

"Aye, m'lady, the practice I have had is well nigh equal, as you say. But, faith, that is not saying there was much of it in either case."

She pouted at the ease with which he parried her thrusts, and turned to find Sir Claude leaning forward with his elbows on the table and his flushed face on his hand, staring impudently at Shale.

"Faith, but he fences well with his tongue, m'lady," he said, with something like a sneer upon his lips.

She smiled sweetly.

"In truth he does, Sir Claude, fully as well as you do with your sword."

He laughed.

"Faith, m'lady, that is saying much, e'en

though I would not brag. Yet, to give Anderley his due, you're no doubt right. Every man to his own weapons."

He stared straight at Shale, but the latter was toying with his wineglass, and seemed not to hear him.

Gloria hurriedly changed the subject by suggesting that the ladies should proceed to the withdrawing room and leave the men to their wine.

This announcement, as was usual on such occasions, was received with shouts of "no, no," from the men, but as was also usual and as was expected of them, the ladies paid no heed to the insincere demands for beauty to remain, and amidst much clamor and bowing and scraping and curtseying, they wended their way to the pink and white drawing room where M'lady Gloria flitted from one chattering group to another superintending the dispensing of tea, and listening tactfully to titbits of the latest London gossip.

Meanwhile, Sir Humphrey, calling loudly for more wine, opened the drinking bout by toasting the health of "M'lady Gloria," the mistress of the Grange.

Amidst shouts of acclamation, the toast was

drunk and, at the call of Sir Claude Aylesbury, it was drunk again.

Then after the company, already well besotted, had seated itself, Sir Brian Bushworthy, of Cavendish Manor, staggered to his feet and, as he had an incurable stutter, he spoke in this wise:

"He-he-he-he-he-he," began his treble voice, but before he could proceed further young Sir Rupert Grimstone, seated in the next chair, burst in.

"What the divil d'ye mean by he-he-he, Bushie? Demme, man, we don't want a laughing song. Shiver me, but you must be merrily drunk."

Sir Brian spluttered.

"I s-said he-he-he——"

"We all know you said he-he-he—but we don't want any more he-he-he's," quoth Sir Rupert amidst much laughter.

Again Sir Brian spluttered.

"Sh-sh-shut up, Grimstone," he roared. "I-I'm proposing a d-d-demmed toast, m-m-man."

"Oh, I s-s-see," mimicked Sir Rupert. "Well, shiver me, get it out Bushie. We don't have all evening to wait for your d-d-demmed toast."

Sir Brian essayed another attempt.

"He-he-here's to the m-man who m-m-marries m'lady-gug-gug-gug-gug——"

Sir Rupert stared at him in mock amazement.

"What's the matter, Bushie, are you drowning? Gadzooks, man, how many times have I told you not to drink so much. Faith, gentlemen, the man's actually drowned himself in punch."

Sir Brian became so maddened that he could restrain himself no longer, and, with a vicious jerk, he pulled Sir Rupert's chair from under him, depositing the young gallant upon the floor where, in most undignified fashion, he sat until a footman hoisted him to his feet.

"Zounds, Bushie, an' it were any other man who played me such a trick, I'd have his b-b-blood. And me simply trying to save you from drowning," he quoth as he helped himself to a liberal dose of punch.

"I wasn't d-d-drowning," roared Sir Brian. "I was proposing the health of the man who marries Lady Gug-gug-Gloria."

Sir Rupert looked surprised, but rose to his feet unsteadily.

"Gentlemen, the toast is one we all would fain acknowledge, but here it is."

All rose to the toast but Sir Claude Aylesbury, who only sipped his wine and looked the while at John Shale, who, however, with a smile on his lips, drained his glass.

The fun waxed fast and furious till a footman whispered in Sir Humphrey's big ear that M'lady Gloria and the ladies would be glad if the gentlemen would join them in a hand at cards.

Upon Sir Humphrey telling the company this, there were loud shouts of "Aye! To the tables. Let's try our luck."

Amidst much scraping of chairs and snapping of snuffboxes, the gentlemen, for the most part somewhat unsteadily, proceeded—some of them arm-in-arm—to the cardroom, where they flopped into the chairs around the tables.

And now Shale would fain have hung back, for he had no great love of gambling, and would much have preferred to have sat and looked at the face of the Lady Gloria, but Sir Claude Aylesbury would not hear of him being left out.

"Faith, man, we've been together all the night. Why split our company now," he said. "Besides I have a wish to see if my luck at cards is equal to thine."

Shale looked at Gloria, who was standing by, and then with a sigh he took his place at the table.

Gloria laughed.

"Why, I never knew you sighed so much,

m'lord, till this night," she said. "Faith, one
would think you were——"

She stopped suddenly, blushed and hastily
covered her confusion by offering to deal the
cards. Shale was looking at her.

"Aye, m'lady, one would almost think I was,"
he replied. "And 'twere but natural, methinks,
m'lady."

She dealt the cards in silence, but her cheeks
were burning, and their color which betokened
the instant effect of Shale's words, made Sir
Claude Aylesbury bite his thin lips, and deepen
the frown upon his already black brow.

"Faith, m'lady, no doubt he is in love," he
said roughly. "But from all I've heard, that is
no uncommon state for him to be in."

Shale lifted his eyes from his cards and stared
full at Aylesbury. The latter returned his stare,
grinning impudently the while.

Lady Gloria felt her cheeks grow pale and her
fingers tighten on the back of Shale's chair
behind which she stood. What would he do?
The eyes of all at the table were upon him.

A grim smile overspread his face. Then with
a light low laugh, he turned to his cards.

"Zounds, Aylesbury, but an' you heard that
your hearing hath need o' vast improvement,"
he said easily.

Aylesbury flushed, and a hot retort sprang to his lips, but ere he could utter it there was a little scream, and a lady flopped into the arms of Sir Brian Bushworthy so suddenly that he staggered and well nigh fell.

It was the Lady Genevieve who, standing near by, had sensed the tragedy in the air, and had resorted to her favorite subterfuge of fainting to divert attention to herself.

"B-b-b me s-s-s-s-," spluttered Sir Brian.

"Your what?" broke in Sir Rupert Grimstone. "You sound as if you'd been drinking soda water, man, 'stead of punch. Lay the lady in a chair afore your breath doth suffocate her."

Shale rose, and gently lifting the Lady Genevieve from Sir Brian's arms, deposited her on a couch where Gloria, vastly relieved at the turn events had taken, plied smelling salts so assiduously that the tears came to Lady Genevieve's eyes, and she had perforce to open them.

Then while the men returned to the tables, the white-haired old lady smiled upon Gloria.

" 'Twas neatly done, was it not?" she whispered.

Gloria smiled.

"A credit to you, dear aunt," she murmured, "and in the nick o' time."

Lady Genevieve nodded wisely.

"Beware of that Sir Claude Aylesbury," she whispered. "I have it from my kitchen maids that he has been boasting openly in the 'Amherst' taproom that he will make you his bride."

Gloria frowned, and bit her pretty lip.

"Have no fear, aunt," she said, "'tis for your precious nephew my own fears are."

Again Lady Genevieve nodded.

"True, Gloria. An' they fight, Aylesbury must win, for is he not the finest swordsman in England, and 'tis said that he wounded Geoffrey already in a duel."

" 'Tis true, Aunt Genevieve. For that reason they must never meet, though 'twill be hard to prevent it for Sir Claude seems bent upon picking a quarrel."

She returned to the table to insure peace, and found Aylesbury more furious than ever since he was losing heavily. She stood behind him for a time, during which he drank several cups of wine and with each mouthful he frowned more deeply at Shale.

The latter, unperturbed by his viciousness, was playing quietly and almost absent-mindedly. His luck was running so that he could not help winning, though he would as soon have lost, for the increasing pile of guineas in front of him gave him no satisfaction.

But now Aylesbury was becoming more and more incapable of controlling his fury at his losses. He forgot that ladies were in the room and swore so deeply that more than once Shale was on the point of calling him to order, and was only prevented from doing so by Gloria's fleeting glance, silently pleading him to say nothing.

After one particularly low oath, however, Sir Rupert Grimstone pushed back his chair.

"Demme, Aylesbury, do you forget that there are women in the room."

"Y-ye-yes," put in Sir Brian Bushworthy, " 'tis time you controlled your w-w-words, Ayle-Ayle-Ayle——"

"Don't call me ale," roared Sir Claude in fury. "What d'ye think I am—a beer-vat?"

At this Gloria giggled, and Sir Claude turned his baneful glare upon her.

"Aye, snigger, m'lady," he growled, "no doubt you're glad to see my money pass into the hands of yon easy-tempered suitor of yours."

Shale sat back quickly.

"Easy tempered is right, Aylesbury," he said grimly. "But, mark me, man, the wrath that's hard to rouse is hard to appease."

An evil light came into Aylesbury's eyes.

"Faith, an' by what right do you champion m'lady?" he sneered.

"By the right of a gentleman, I hope," quoth Shale, gently taking a sip of his wine. " 'Tis plain you must beware how you address a lady in my company, friend."

Aylesbury leaned forward, and picked up his wine glass. It was half full, and he held it poised in his hand for a second the while he glared at Shale.

Then with a quick movement he jerked the crimson liquid across the table full at John Shale's face.

The latter's hand was on his own glass at the time, and there was a tinkling crash as he snapped the delicate stem.

Gloria gave a little gasp of horror, then stopped, staring as if fascinated at the wine trickling from Shale's forehead across his face.

He was still smiling, but there was a steely glitter in his blue eyes.

Without a word he withdrew from his pocket the silk kerchief in which m'lady's roses were wrapped and, raising it to his face, wiped the wet from it.

Dead silence was in the room.

All eyes were fixed upon the two men. Aylesbury's action could have but one ending, and all waited the speaking of the words which would proclaim the coming of the duel.

· Now Shale rose slowly and steadily to his feet, and bowed before the Lady Gloria.

"M'lady, it grieves me sore that your house should be the scene of such a squabble as this, and more so that you yourself should be a witness o't. Pray, m'lady, may I crave that you withdraw, and take with you these other gentle dames. Sir Claude Aylesbury and myself have a little business to arrange."

Gloria stood white-faced for a moment, then burst out passionately:

"Is there no other way. Cannot an apology be made—oh, if 'tis anything I have done—if my laughing annoyed you, Sir Claude, direct your attack at me, and interfere not with others, for——"

She stopped suddenly at a motion from Shale.

"An attack directed at you would have the same result, m'lady," he said in a very low voice. "Sir Rupert, will you and Sir Brian Bushworthy hold converse with Sir Claude Aylesbury's seconds on my behalf."

Gloria gave a little gasp of despair, and in a helpless sort of way, took the arm Shale graciously offered her.

"You honor us, m'lord," said Sir Rupert.

"Sir Claude, will you please appoint two gentlemen to act for you, and we will arrange this
matter with despatch, so that the evening's play
may not be spoiled."

Aylesbury bowed, smiling evilly.

"One hour after dawn on the piece of sward
in front of Sir Humphrey's hunting-box—with
rapiers," he said. "Sir Humphrey and Sir
Gerald Mortlake will act for me."

A gleam of satisfaction lit up Sir Humphrey's
face.

"Aye, we'll act for you right willingly,
Aylesbury," he growled.

"So be it," grimly said Sir Rupert. "And
may the best man win."

LADY GENEVIEVE DISPLAYS A LITTLE PARDONABLE
PRIDE

JUST inside the door of the portrait galleries,
Lady Gloria and John Shale paused.

The long lines of ancestors looked down
grimly upon her fragile little form standing
beside the great broad figure of the new Lord
Anderley.

"Why did you do it?" she gasped. "Oh, why
did you do it?"

He smiled ruefully.

"I'faith, m'lady, when a man throws wine in
my face, what else is there for me to do?"

She stamped her little foot in vexation.

"I know—I know. You could do nothing else.
But 'twas all my fault. I giggled when Sir Brian
called him 'ale.'"

"I do not blame you, m'lady. The term fitted
so well, y'know."

She tried to smile, but failed. There were
tears in her eyes when she looked up at him.

"He is a wonderful fencer."

Shale bowed.

173

"So 'tis said, m'lady, so 'tis said."

She looked at him sharply.

"You ought to know. You fought him before."

He sighed.

"So 'tis said, m'lady, so 'tis said."

Again she stamped her tiny foot.

"Can't you say anything else than 'so 'tis said'?"

He smiled.

"Aye, m'lady, but there's nothing more required."

She pouted.

"You know he can fence better than you?" she demanded.

"So 'tis said—er, I mean, very possibly he can, m'lady."

"Well knowing that, why did you challenge him?"

"Nay, m'lady, he challenged me—I did but take up the challenge and wipe the wine from my face with—with the kerchief which contained your roses, m'lady."

The tears started to her eyes again.

"Then why—why not fight with pistols—you would stand a better chance."

He shook his head.

"Nay, m'lady, I know but little of these newfangled contraptions. I pin my faith to steel and, if it fail me, to the thickness of my skin."

She looked away hopelessly, then suddenly she turned to him and laid her hand upon his arm.

"Please don't fight," she said suddenly.

He looked down at her with soft love shining in his eyes.

"Dear lady, it grieves me sore to refuse you even one request. Ask of me what you will save only that, and thy wish shall be granted."

She looked up at him, and her face was very close to his.

"For—for my sake," she pleaded.

He drew his breath sharply.

"M'lady," he murmured in anguish tone, "dear m'lady, tempt—tempt me not."

She looked at him for one second and though her eyes were dimmed with tears, they gleamed out admiration.

"Then if you needs must fight, may God fight with you. And fight for me—my lord."

She bowed her head that he might not see her tears and, as she stood thus, he bent above her and his lips barely touched the golden curls, while his hands rose as if to take them amongst his fingers.

And so they were standing when the Lady Genevieve found them.

She looked at them white-faced and red-eyed, but with pride gleaming in her sweet old face.

"My children," she whispered brokenly, "I have been looking everywhere for you."

They turned and gazed at her silently. Gloria's face was red with blushes. Shale's was very white.

"It is no use, aunt," said Gloria weakly. "He must fight."

Lady Genevieve smiled.

"I know it. You see, Gloria, he is an Anderley. A true Anderley, born and bred an Anderley."

Shale laughed.

"Faith, m'lady—I mean aunt dear—'tis an honor to be an Anderley since you are one. But why these red eyes? I am not dead yet, and, zounds, I have no intention of dying. So spare your sweet selves these worries, and remember that 'tis only said Sir Claude is England's finest swordsman, and it hath yet to be proved."

"But he fought you already, didn't he?" said Gloria, looking at him queerly.

He started, and sighed again.

"Ah, so 'tis said, m'lady, so 'tis said."

She stared at him a long time, then turned and walked slowly away. And as she did so,

Shale's eyes followed her wonderingly. Then once more he sighed, and turned to Lady Genevieve.

"Wilt let me lead you to the withdrawing room?" he murmured. "Methinks my presence will be needed shortly, and I fain would snatch a few hours sleep, the better to be refreshed."

Two minutes later, Lady Genevieve repeated his words proudly to an admiring circle of petticoats.

"Sleep, ladies!" she said. "Fancy that! The coolness of the man to think of sleeping with such an ordeal on his mind. But then, dears, he is an Anderley, isn't he?"

" 'Tis wonderful," sighed Lady Bushworthy. "And my poor Brian is as excited as a bride on her wedding day, and him only a second. Law, I wonder when he'll ever fight a duel. He never is any more than a second, and 'tis strange that his man always gets killed. Law! I didn't mean to upset you, Lady Genevieve. Only 'tis strange, isn't it?"

"No, it isn't strange at all," broke in a quiet little voice, and all eyes turned to see Lady Gloria standing white-faced in the doorway. "It's perfectly natural. Because in the past Sir Brian has seconded only half-tipsy brawlers. But to-night he acts for a man—a real man."

"For an Anderley," put in Lady Genevieve.
"Quite right, my dear."

But Gloria only looked at her silently for a
long time, then turned away.

TWO PLOTTERS HEAR LIGHT FOOTSTEPS ON
THE STAIR

JUST as the first streaks of dawn darted
through, Sir Claude Aylesbury and Sir
Humphrey Clayville passed down the great staircase of Clayville Grange and entered the dark,
deserted card-room.

Sir Humphrey carried a candle, and this he set
on one of the card tables.

Then, in the dimness of the solitary light, the
two men filled out small glasses of brandy and
drank it neat.

"Here's to your success i' the fight," said Sir
Humphrey, "though, faith, 'tis assured."

Sir Claude grinned evilly.

"Aye, 'tis assured egad," he growled. "And
when I have carried out my part of the bargain,
don't you forget yours. I've shown you how easy
it is for me to pick a quarrel."

Sir Humphrey swore, and hastily assured him
that he would not fail him.

"You kill Anderley," he added, "and I'll see
that the wench weds you. 'Tis a matter of small

179

account to me who she weds so long as she does
not wed Anderley. My brother's will puts it
that she must marry him 'ere this year is out, or
the estates pass to me. The fool, he might as
well have given me them right away and saved
me ridding the earth of Anderley's carcass."

"Well, it matters not," growled Aylesbury. "I
only wish I'd finished the fellow when last I
fought him, but that is of small account. I like
his impudence and cool cheek so little that 'twill
give me most extreme pleasure to spit him on the
end of my sword. Your request for me to pick a
quarrel with him was well nigh useless, for,
despite it, I would have issued him a challenge."

"What's that?" suddenly gasped Sir Humphrey, quickly springing to his feet.

There was the sound of light footsteps in the
hall outside, the footsteps of some one running
swiftly up the stairs.

Sir Humphrey emitted a string of deep curses.

"Some one was out there in the hall," he muttered. "What if they have heard us?"

Sir Claude made a gesture of disdain.

"Well, what if they have, dolt? It matters not
whether a quarrel is planned or not so long as
it is a quarrel, and as such it must be settled."

Sir Humphrey cursed again, then stamped
towards the door.

"I will go and get that fool Mortlake," he said. "He was in a drunken slumber when last I saw him. An' he wakens not I'll throw him a bucket o' cold water across his besotted pow."

Sir Claude laughed easily.

"Gadzooks! Sir Humphrey, an' you do you'll be getting yourself in a brawl next, an' Sir Gerald Mortlake could pink you as easily as he could take a pinch o' snuff."

Again Sir Humphrey swore, and, swearing, stamped heavily up the stairs.

And, hearing him, the Lady Gloria fled down the corridor and crashed into some one who came out of a room.

He stood with his arms about her, looking down at her.

"Faith," he murmured, "I'm fated to meet you thus in the dark, it seems, m'lady."

She lay a moment in his arms, then drew back.

"You go to meet him?" she whispered.

"Aye, m'lady," he replied, in a low voice.

A little shudder shook her frame.

"May the good God go with you," she said.

"Amen!" he added, fervently.

For a moment they stood; then she leaned forward to him.

"If—if you care—you—you may kiss—me— once."

She heard him take his breath in quickly, then something like a sob broke from him.

"Dear m'lady," he whispered brokenly. "Dear m'lady."

She raised her head, and he touched her white brow for an instant with his lips.

Then she stood aside to let him pass.

"Good-by," she whispered.

He smiled softly in the darkness.

"Nay, nay, dear m'lady. Let it be *au-revoir.*"

A moment later she was standing alone watching his great manly figure fading into the silent gloom of the corridor.

She heard him meet Sir Rupert Grimstone and Sir Brian Bushworthy at the top of the staircase. The latter's treble voice was raised in peevish protest at his being aroused so early.

"D-d-demme, Anderley, I admire you most f-f-fervently, b-b-but I wish you'd fight your d-d-duels i' the d-d-d-d——"

"Dark," suggested Sir Rupert.

"N-no-no—not d-dark—in the d-d-d——"

"Drawing-room," ventured the other sarcastically.

"Sh-shut up, y-you fool," quoth the wrathful Bushworthy, "I m-mean in the d-d——"

"Oh, never mind what you mean, Bushie," broke in Rupert. "Let's get on with the duel."

"Ye-ye-you're a callous b-b-brute, Grimstone, d-d-dragging a m-m-man out of his b-b-bed to see a duel which should have been f-fought in the d-d-d——"

"If you d-d-d-didder there any more I'll hit you over the h-h-head," said Sir Rupert.

"D-d-daytime," gasped Sir Brian.

Sir Rupert looked out through the casement at the breaking dawn.

"Almost," he said.

Sir Brian spluttered.

"I meant f-fought in the d-d-daytime."

Sir Rupert swore deeply.

"Gad, Bushie, if you don't learn to speak with your hands like the Frenchies do, I'll be the death of you. It's more than I can make out how you ever came to propose to your wife."

Sir Brian frowned.

"I did-didn't," he gasped, "sh-she p-p-proposed to me."

At this Sir Rupert roared with laughter and Shale chuckled aloud, so that Sir Humphrey, listening, stared at them in amaze ere he uneasily went on his way to meet Sir Claude and Sir Gerald Mortlake.

Lady Gloria was about to tiptoe after him when she was arrested by the sound of a merry whistle coming from the room whence John Shale had emerged a few seconds before.

For a moment she hesitated, then she pushed open the door and entered.

In the dim morning light she saw a figure standing over a chair busily engaged neatly folding up clothes of various hues and textures.

"Peter," she said severely.

The man gave a sudden start and swung round while the whistling ceased with a jerk.

"Zookers, m'lady, what a fright you did give me, an' I may say so, m'lady."

"Peter," still more severely.

Peter tugged his forelock.

"Yes, m'lady."

"I'm surprised at you, Peter."

He elevated his eyebrows.

"Surprised at me, ma'am—zookers!"

"Yes, Peter, surprised and disappointed."

"For why, m'lady?"

"Peter, you were whistling just now."

Peter moved uneasily.

"To be sure I was, m'lady."

"And do you know where your master is, Peter?"

"I—I do, m'lady. He's gone to do a bit of dueling, I hear. They're going to get a fine morning for it."

She stamped her little foot.

"You talk about it as if it were a sport like hunting or riding."

"So it is, m'lady."

Again she stamped her foot.

"You're very wicked, Peter. Don't you know your master may be killed. And I thought you loved him."

Peter's brow cleared, and a broad grin overspread his features.

"Zookers, m'lady, is that what's worrying you. I thought 'twas summat serious."

She frowned.

"It is serious—very serious. I said he might be killed. You ought to be away looking after him."

"Me! m'lady. Bless you, he don't need no looking after. He can look after hisself all right —by zookers, he can."

She smiled wanly.

"But Sir Claude is such a good fencer."

Peter winked, and tried to look very impressive.

"Aye, m'lady, but tell me, have you seen the master fence?"

"No, Peter."

"Then, m'lady, you go along now and get the

treat of your life, m'lady. And don't you be a-feared for m'lord no more."

She looked hopefully at him.

"I hope you're right, Peter."

"Zookers, ma'am, 'tain't often I am, but there's times when I couldn't be wrong, even if I tried."

Gloria turned to the door and opened it. Seeing this, Peter called after her——

"And that's why I was whistling, m'lady."

She passed out and as she ran along the corridor, she heard again that merry tune ring blithely out.

Meanwhile, Shale, a grim smile upon his lips, passed slowly down the great staircase, followed closely by Sir Brian and Sir Rupert.

The latter carried three rapiers in his right hand. He and Sir Brian had become silent, as befitted the seriousness of the mission upon which they were bound.

Out into the breaking morning light they passed, walking across the springy turf with heavy tread. As they passed through the little wood that bounded the hunting lodge, they heard the sound of footsteps on the leaves and twigs ahead of them, and they knew that Sir Claude Aylesbury and his seconds were up to time.

They did not think of looking back, but had they done so, they might have seen a slight girlish figure picking dainty steps amongst the underbrush.

The Lady Gloria was determined that she should witness the duel.

"Perhaps there will be need for me," she told herself. "If he is but wounded, I may be able to tend him."

But even as she thought this her heart misgave her, for she knew that Aylesbury would never spare Lord Anderley if he could help it. Besides, was the whole duel not prearranged by Sir Humphrey? She bit her little lips as she thought of her uncle's perfidy.

Sir Claude and Sir Humphrey were in close conversation when Shale and his seconds arrived at the scene of the duel—a little green sward about twenty yards square, bordered by trees on three sides and by the Hunting Lodge on the fourth. The door of the lodge was open, but the place was unoccupied save by some pheasants which scattered with much flapping of wings at the approach of the men.

Sir Claude bowed stiffly to Shale, then proceeded to remove his coat, and tuck up the sleeves of his silk shirt.

Shale gravely did the same, after which he selected a rapier from the three Sir Rupert carried. With great care he tested its poise, strength and spring, bending it well nigh double ere he was satisfied that it could stand the supreme test to which it was about to be subjected.

"A pretty blade," quoth Sir Rupert. "'Twas my father's!"

"The finest I've ever trifled with," responded Shale, "and worthy of your noble sire."

"Thanks, Anderley, I only hope it serves you well this morn."

There was silence for a second. Both men were ready and were but breathing deep the fresh morning air before opening the bout.

"W-will you have a snuff, m'lord," ventured Sir Brian, who alone amongst them all was quivering with excitement.

"'Tis an honor," said Shale, gallantly.

"Demme, Bushie," broke in Sir Rupert, "you're sprinkling the whole lawn with your filthy snuff. Can't you keep your hand steady, man. Faith, ye'd think 'twas you was fighting this duel."

Shale laughed heartily as he helped himself to a small pinch of the brown powder. His laughter seemed to grate upon Sir Claude's nerves, for he frowned fiercely, and gave Sir Humphrey a nasty rap over the knuckles with his rapier by letting it spring back suddenly.

"Ow!" yelled Sir Humphrey. "By gad, Aylesbury, you're devilish careless with that blade of yours."

Aylesbury grinned viciously.

"Aye, so I am reputed to be, man. Devilish careless, i'faith."

He swung round suddenly and faced Shale.

"Now, m'lord. Art ready?"

Shale dusted the last fragments of snuff from his finger tips with his silk kerchief. As he did so, two crumbled rose buds dropped upon the sward.

Instantly he stooped and picking them up with his left hand raised them to his lips.

Then, with them still dangling between his fingers, he brought his blade to the salute.

"On guard," rasped out Aylesbury, 'tween clenched teeth, and like a flash of light the rapiers flew round and rang one upon the other.

REVEALS HOW ROSES CHANGE COLOR

A S the two men faced one another, the sun was darting its warming rays through the skies, and these fell upon the steel of the swords, causing them to flash and glitter like a myriad of flaming lights.

Aylesbury fought with the ease and confidence of a master of the art. He sprang nimbly from one side to the other, parrying Shale's thrusts with a supercilious smile upon his lips. He was never in one place for an instant, but pressed his attacks, first from the left, then from the right, now from the center, sometimes low, sometimes high, always fiercely and with masterly strength and skill.

Shale stood immovable save for his right arm and keen blue eyes. His face was grim, but then it was always grim, more or less, and withal he did not appear to be greatly in fear of his opponent. His left hand, from which dangled the two tantalizing roses, was held gracefully poised slightly above his head. Aylesbury fought with his left arm well out of the way behind his back.

Three times Sir Claude thrust viciously at that graceful hand, but on the first two occasions his weapon was turned aside with swift surety by the other's ceaselessly circling blade, and on the third he narrowly escaped being pinked on the right knee himself by a swift lunge from Shale. After this, Sir Claude decided to forget about the left arm, as such a high attack left too many openings.

Now, however, the smile of easy confidence had disappeared from his face.

'Twas plain Anderley had improved vastly in his fencing since last he fought him and indeed he seemed to fight with a different style altogether. He had become an infinitely more formidable opponent. His wrist seemed tremendously powerful, and one twist of it nearly wrenched Aylesbury's blade from his firm grasp.

Standing stolidly as he did, too, displayed the confidence of an experienced swordsman, sure of his ability to turn aside the fiercest thrusts of his opponent. He was obviously conserving his strength for the time when Aylesbury, worn out by his constant leaping about the green sward, should falter in his fencing, and perhaps leave an easy opening.

Still Sir Claude knew his own ability, and now he no longer thought of playing with his opponent like a cat plays with a mouse, as at first had been his intention, but flung himself into a new fierce attack with all the wonderful power at his command.

His blade flashed past Shale's shoulder like a streak of light, and was turned aside from his breast in the nick of time. Now it drove ruthlessly at his heart and actually ripped a jagged tear in the silken shirt. Then it darted viciously at that strong powerful sword arm, and sliding down Slade's blade with a rasping shriek took the skin off his knuckles.

Shale's lips tightened a trifle, and his square jaw went forward still further. That was all. He did not make a motion otherwise, save only that his sword arm seemed to move faster than ever—if that were possible.

Suddenly Lady Gloria, watching through the branches and leaves of a big bush on the edge of the sward, gave a little gasp of horror and closed her eyes.

Aylesbury's blade had leaped forward from guard straight at Shale's heart. The latter, attacking at the time, was just a fraction of a second too late.

"My God!" gasped Rupert.

For the first time Shale's body moved. He seemed to drop to earth, then like a bullet from a pistol, his blade darted up and clinked against the other's.

Again that shirt was ripped open, this time from the breast down to the left elbow, and a deep streak of red blood showed where it had torn the surface of the skin upon its course. This done, it rent a jagged hole in the white bare arm and darted back on guard.

An instant's pause, then Shale stood upright again without even deigning to glance at the wound. His arm now hung limply by his side, but already he was pressing the attack upon Sir Claude. The latter, feeling he had scored a point, was somewhat unprepared and fell back. The wonderful rapidity with which Shale's steel darted hither and thither, however, quickly brought him to his senses, and desperately he endeavored once more to assume the offensive.

But now his opponent's eyes were narrowed to pin points and glittering even as his blade, and 'twas as much as Aylesbury could do to save himself from being pinked on more than one occasion.

Gloria, watching from the edge of the glade, seemed fascinated by the red blood trickling down Shale's left arm. She saw that he still held in his hand the white rosebuds she had given him, but his fingers were very limp. The blood, too, had reached their tips, and now the petals of the flowers were dyed crimson.

All this Gloria, with tears in her eyes, observed ere her attention was once more drawn to the whirling steel that alone separated the two men.

Sir Claude Aylesbury was on defense and, like every true swordsman, he knew it. His face was white and tense. Despite the fact that he had drawn blood, he was fully aware that he was fighting for his life. This was a new Lord Anderley who faced him. No longer could he play with him in any way he pleased. No longer could he deceive him with the cunning tricks he had become the master of. He was fighting a man who knew as much as he did. Nay, he was fighting a man who knew more.

Instinctively he felt that the other had not put his full skill into his play till now. Shale's blade seemed to be everywhere at once—now it was searching for an opening—now it found one and darted in, only to be turned aside in the nick of time.

Aylesbury felt his face grow pale. He knew that the blood was fading from it. It was his own life that was at stake now—not the other man's. He tried every subterfuge at his command, he played every trick he knew, but each effort failed to pierce that shield of steel that whirled about him ruthlessly and determinedly.

There was no gainsaying it. Some time, soon, very soon, it would break through his guard no matter how desperately he might combat it.

Gloria, staring fascinated, felt the blood slowly flood her cheeks again. A swordswoman herself, an expert with the rapier, she knew as well as did Sir Claude, and Sir Humphrey, and Sir Rupert, that the advantage was now with Shale.

True, her heart was filled with misgivings. Perhaps Aylesbury was but playing a trick upon his opponent. Perhaps he was only waiting for a suitable opening. Yet that look in his eyes— that telltale pallor of his face did not indicate a reserve of skill.

Shale was pale, too—but his was the pallor due to loss of blood. It was not the whiteness of a man fighting to spare his own life.

Gloria saw that the white roses she had given to Peter the morning before were red roses now, and a great lump rose in her throat. It was his blood that dyed them.

Suddenly Shale's guard dropped. Gloria gave a cry—a wail of despair. He seemed exhausted, his sword was upon the ground. There was

nothing now for Sir Claude to do but to plunge
his rapier into his heart.

Gloria's pulse seemed to stop beating—she
stared fascinated at the men.

Like an arrow from a bow, Aylesbury's blade
leapt at John Shale's heart, driven straight and
true with all the strength at the command of a
powerful man.

There was a flash of steel in the sunlight—a
grinding, rasping ring of metal upon metal—a
moan from Sir Rupert, then a desperate wail
from Sir Claude and a low, soft, long drawn
"Ah-h!" from Shale.

When Gloria opened her eyes once more she
could scarce believe their very sight.

For John Shale stood still upon the green
sward, his left hand—that left hand all had
thought so useless—clasped firmly round the
rapier of Sir Claude Aylesbury. And his own
blade?

It quivered menacingly within a fraction of an
inch of the throat of "England's finest fencer."

There was dead silence—a silence as of the
grave—and still the deadly point of that ruthless
steel shimmered within an ace of Aylesbury's
throat.

Terror was written in the man's eyes now; his
face was ghastly. He tugged feebly at his sword,

but without avail. It remained perfectly still in the grip of that bloody left hand.

Then with a sudden jerk, Shale wrested it from his grasp and threw it upon the ground.

This done, he lowered his own weapon and, with a stiff bow to his opponent, turned away.

Sir Claude stood staring at him with unbelieving eyes for a second, then he suddenly seemed to crumple up and, with a little moan, sank to the ground in a faint.

Shale looked at him with something like contempt, ere he caught sight of Lady Gloria standing motionless at the edge of the glade.

He frowned a little and hastily turned to Sir Rupert, who stood somewhat dazed.

"My coat, man," he muttered. "Dost not observe m'lady. Hide me this wound an' you would save me much explanation."

Sir Rupert grabbed his coat and helped him into it, breathing forth praises of his skill the while.

" 'Twas wonderful, m'lord," he vouched. "Something I've ne'er seen in my life afore. 'Twas skill of the first quality."

Here Sir Brian broke in, stuttering, as usual.

"T-the only p-p-pity of it is that you d-d-did not k-k-kill him."

"You bloodthirsty wretch," smiled Shale as he

turned to greet M'lady Gloria, who was slowly crossing to them.

She stood with face very white gazing up at him.

"Ah, m'lord."

"Aye, m'lady."

" 'Tis over, m'lord?"

"Aye, m'lady."

"And still you live, m'lord?"

"Aye, m'lady."

With tears in her eyes——

"God is good, m'lord?"

"Aye, m'lady."

"You're sorely wounded?"

" 'Tis but a scratch, m'lady."

"Wilt suffer me to bind it for thee?"

"Nay, m'lady, 'tis of small account."

"Come with me to the house at once."

He looked down at Aylesbury, now recovering from his swoon.

"I will, m'lady, but first I would gather me up that which is mine."

"What mean you, m'lord?"

He smiled quizzically down at her and then turning, indicated Aylesbury's sword.

And now looking, Gloria saw sticking on the point, two roses blood-red in color.

Sir Claude's last fierce thrust had succeeded

only in passing through their sweet-scented hearts.

She stooped and gently withdrew them from the steel. As she did so, Aylesbury moved and sat up suddenly.

"In—in truth, a very wonderful display, m'lord," he muttered feebly. "An' I may say it. But prithee where did'st learn the knack of that last trick o' yours?"

Shale smiled grimly.

"An' it please you, sir—'twas my greatest heritage."

Aylesbury contrived a wry smile.

"Faith, then it was a goodly one, for only one man do I know who could employ that trick in sword play, and that man was not your father, Lord Anderley. Nay, rather was he the man who fled with your father's sister."

Shale went a little pale and turned away rather hastily. He seemed to feel Gloria's eyes fixed upon him in silent questioning, but he deliberately averted his own and moved towards the wooded path leading to the house.

In the shadow of the trees he paused and looked down at the slim figure of the girl who walked by his side.

"My lady, these roses in your hand are mine!"

She looked down at them tenderly.

"And what would you do with them?"

"I would treasure them in memory of you."

She gazed far away into the wood, and then in soft voice:

"But why so, m'lord, when thou hast me here myself?"

The red blood rushed to his cheeks. His right arm seized her almost roughly.

"Ah—ah—m'lady, m'lady—dear m'lady."

She raised her face to his.

"M'lord—m'lord—Geoffrey."

He stared down at her in dazed sort of fashion. The name sounded strange upon his ears. It seemed to carry dull, heart-breaking realization in its train.

Then once more his eyes saw only the fairness of her face, the glory of her hair, the beauty of her lips. He bent his head——

Suddenly a voice rang out.

"Egad, Bushie, but we seem to have happened on a love affair even at this odd hour. Faith, 'tis early to go a-wooing."

Sir Rupert stood grinning a couple of yards away from them.

Sir Brian spluttered. He always had to splutter before he could speak.

"It's t-too d-d-demned early to w-woo. I'm g-going back to b-b-b-b——"

"Breakfast," ventured Sir Rupert.

"N-no, to b-b-b——"

"Bury yourself," tried Sir Rupert again.

"N-n-no, to b-b-bed," gasped Sir Brian.

"Ah, same thing, Bushie—same thing. I'll come with you."

HOMAGE IS DONE TO A HERO

L ADY GLORIA sat upon the table of the still deserted breakfast room.

John Shale occupied a chair in front of her. His wounded arm reposed comfortably in m'lady's lap, the better for her to proceed with the bathing and bandaging of it.

The door of the breakfast room was closed and several chairs were thrust against it to prevent any one from entering.

From outside came the sound of many voices clamoring for admission.

Gloria looked down at Shale.

"They are all wanting to congratulate you, Geoffrey."

He smiled.

" 'Tis beyond my understanding, m'lady."

She pouted.

"When will you cease to call me m'lady, Geoffrey?"

He gazed away out through the casement.

"I know not when, m'lady. Perchance when you cease to call me Geoffrey."

She stopped bandaging his arm, and looked at him suddenly.

"Whatever do you mean, Geoffrey. What am I to call you. Surely you don't want me to call you m'lord."

He suddenly realized what he had said.

"Nay, nay, m'lady. In very sooth I do not."

She resumed her mission of mercy once more.

"Ah, then, perhaps, you would like me to call you Geoffrey—dear?"

He blushed and laughed.

"In truth 'tis vastly better than the other, m'lady."

She worked on in silence till, the bandaging completed, she tied a kerchief in a neat sling, and putting it round his neck, gently placed the wounded arm within it.

"Geoffrey," she said suddenly.

"Aye, m'lady."

"Do you know that there is something very strange about you?"

He tried to look surprised.

"Zounds, m'lady, but that's the first I've heard o't."

She heeded him not.

"Yes, there's something very strange about you, and I want you to tell me what it all means."

He moved uneasily.

"Prithee, how can I tell you, m'lady, when I know not what you mean yourself."

She pondered.

"Well, there was that meeting of yours in the highway near Sevenoaks. You were clad in very ordinary garments then, not at all like those you have been wearing since."

He laughed.

"Faith, 'tis not unnatural to travel in rough clothes."

She looked at him keenly, and he had to avert his eyes.

"Then you arrived at the Hall on a horse, and accompanied by Peter, a very long time after I saw you. And when I was with you, you were on foot and alone."

Again he laughed, but 'twas a little forced.

"Gad, m'lady, I had just left the inn near by, having heard your cry for help."

She looked thoughtful.

"Then, there's your fencing," she went on. "Once Sir Claude Aylesbury could outmatch you, but now you are easily his master."

" 'Tis the result of much training by a French fencing master, m'lady."

She looked relieved.

"Ah, one who was friendly with he who stole your father's sister from the French Court."

Shale flushed.

"I believe he was, m'lady. But why this questioning? I understand it not. You make me feel like a poacher before a magistrate."

She laughed and clasped his face between her hands.

"You poor boy—why, I was only wondering how these things came about, and in very truth I am mightily pleased to find that you are not really as bad as Dame Rumor hath painted you."

"Why," he asked. "Hath she painted me very black then, m'lady?"

She looked away.

"Yes, Geoffrey, but she is a lady of much imagination, and so I believe not in her."

He stooped and kissed her hand.

"I thank you, m'lady."

At that instant the babel of voices outside increased, and finally a desperate thrust at the door pushed aside the chairs and left the entrance clear.

Lady Genevieve darted nimbly into the room.

"Bless me, children, why ever are you barricading yourselves in this strange fashion. Dost not know the maids are awaiting to get them at the breakfast table?"

"I was but binding up m'lord's wound," said Gloria demurely.

Lady Genevieve looked from one to the other wisely.

"And do you not know that I am much more skilled in that art than you are, child?"

"Nay, nay," protested Shale. "See, she has got me most completely bound up. Faith, I don't know how I am going to get me a pinch of snuff an' I want one."

Lady Genevieve smiled tenderly.

"Every one is waiting to congratulate you on your success in the duel," she said. "And we are all most greatly delighted to know that neither you nor Sir Claude have been killed."

Shale laughed.

"Faith, m'lady, duels are much like characters. They are not nearly so black as they are painted."

Gloria flushed, but Lady Genevieve only leaned forward and kissed Shale, much it may be said to his surprise and embarrassment.

Suddenly a familiar voice broke in.

"Th-there he is, g-gentlemen. The h-h-hero of the hour."

Sir Brian marched into the room at the head of the other guests, who speedily formed a circle round Shale.

"I was his s-s-second," proclaimed Sir Brian proudly. "The f-f-first fight I've ever w-w-won."

"Law!" exclaimed his wife. "I thought you would never be on the winning side, Brian. However did you contrive it?"

" 'Twas not he contrived it, ma'am," said Sir Rupert, glaring disdainfully at his fellow-second. " 'Twas an inordinate stroke of luck he had in being chosen to accompany my humble self. And even then he grumbled so vastly at being pulled out o' bed at sunrise that we well nigh left him behind. And, in sooth, 'twould have mattered little an' we did."

" 'Tis f-f-false," cried Sir Brian, "I only said that duels should be f-f-fought in the d-d-d——"

"He means daytime, gentlemen," put in Sir Rupert, "that's his way of saying daytime. I know, because he told me so this morning."

"If you insult me any more, Grimstone, I'll ch-ch-challenge you to a d-d-d-duel myself."

"Nay, nay, gentlemen," said Shale, laughingly. "There's been enough o' fighting for a day. Let us be merry for a change."

A chorus of voices broke out in agreement, and for a moment there was a babel of sound, every one trying to speak at once.

Then suddenly they subsided and a deadly silence prevailed.

All eyes were turned to the doorway. There, framed in the light of the hall beyond, stood Sir Claude Aylesbury and Sir Humphrey Clayville.

Sir Claude's face was white as death. He bowed stiffly to the company.

"Ah, a pretty gathering, in sooth," he said with a weak smile, "and well worthy of its purpose— to do honor to my conqueror."

He bowed again, and Shale politely returned the salutation.

Sir Claude, with an elaborate flourish, took a pinch of snuff from his gold box and passed it open to Shale.

The latter, with his one free hand, sampled its contents.

"A pleasant morn," quoth Sir Claude.

"In very truth," acknowledged Shale.

"It grieves me that I must hie me back to my own poor place at Otford."

"Nay, not so soon, I trow," put in Sir Humphrey.

Sir Claude waved his hand airily.

"Aye, there is a matter o' small importance which requires my attention, and so must I bid you all adieu. But ere I depart, M'lady Gloria, may I have your promise to join me in a fox hunt on the morrow?"

Gloria looked at Shale, then curtseyed gracefully.

"With pleasure, Sir Claude, an' I have permission to bring my guests along with me?"

Sir Claude bowed.

" 'Tis an honor I but ill deserve," he said in low voice, "and one I shall remember ever if M'lord Anderley and the others o' the company will join me in the chase."

Shale held out his hand instantly.

"The honor is mine, friend," he said. "Though this poor arm which you so neatly pinked this morning may make me ride most gingerly."

Sir Claude took his hand and clasped it warmly, seeing which Sir Humphrey turned away in ill-concealed disgust.

"Why, uncle, aren't you glad everything has ended so happily?" called Gloria.

He turned and glared back at Shale.

"G-r-r-r," he growled, and stamped furiously down the hall.

SURPRISES EVERYBODY

JOHN SHALE spent the day as in a dream. Constantly he was by the side of the Lady Gloria and with every passing moment he realized more deeply the sweetness of her nature and the beauty of her character.

She extracted a thorn from the foot of one of the hounds as tenderly as she had bound up his arm that morning.

The brute was obviously in great pain, but it stood quietly while she performed the little operation, and licked her hand, when she had finished.

"Ah, m'lady, if only more women had the tenderness that you possess, we poor men would be much better creatures," said Shale.

She laughed merrily.

"Well, Geoffrey, in truth you seem to be improving rapidly, at least judging from what Aunt Genevieve tells me. She says that you are vastly better than you were when last you were at home, and from all I heard of you then, I verily believe that she is right."

He smiled ruefully.

"Faith, I know she is," he said. "For I feel I have improved so much that even now I could scarce bring myself to deceive a soul."

She looked up at him tenderly.

"I know you couldn't, Geoffrey."

He turned away so that she would not see the look of pain in his face.

Never had his task seemed so hard. Never had he been so near confessing all.

He walked by her side through the gardens to the edge of a wooded path. There they paused and he gravely accepted the flowers she plucked for him.

"M'lady," he said suddenly. "Have you the roses which I held through the duel this morning?"

She looked down.

"Yes, m'lord."

"Hast forgotten they are mine?"

She shook her head.

"Nay, m'lord, 'tis for that reason that I keep them."

"You keep them, m'lady. Tell me where. I see them not."

She looked up at him, with dimmed eyes.

"They—they are lying close to my heart, m'lord."

He drew a deep breath and closed his eyes to shut out the allurement of her presence, lest he should forget that he was John Shale, and crush her in his arms.

She gazed up wistfully at him, and now the fingers of his strong right hand twitched.

"Ah, m'lady, m'lady," he whispered brokenly. "An' I could but speak—an' I could but speak."

His arm went about her. She leaned so close to him that he could smell the entrancing scent of her hair, that beautiful golden hair, and her face was almost against his shoulder.

Then suddenly there was a hoarse shout behind them and a woman's scream rent the air.

Gloria gave a cry of horror, and Shale swung round quickly.

"My God," he gasped.

Plunging through the beds of blooming flowers towards them was a man. His face was covered with dust and flushed with running.

The sweat streamed down from his forehead, leaving dirty smudges where he had dashed it aside.

His hair was disheveled, and his rough coat was ripped open where some one had grabbed at it.

He was literally foaming at the mouth, and in his hand he held a huge ugly-looking jackknife, which he flourished as he ran straight towards Shale.

Close behind him with grim set face, on which consternation was written, raced Peter at the head of a host of the guests.

"Run, m'lord," he shouted wildly. "Run for your life—for your life."

Shale gave one sweep of his arm and with it thrust Lady Gloria away behind him into the flowers.

Next instant the man with the knife was upon him.

There was a hoarse yell of triumph, the flash of steel in the sunlight, then a sickening thud.

The man's hand went back with a jerk as Shale's fist struck him full on the jaw. His yell ended in a low moan, and he fell back headlong, while his knife whistled through the air and clattered at Gloria's feet.

Shale stood looking down at the man lying on the ground.

"Are you hurt, master?—are you hurt?" cried Peter in anguish, racing up to him.

Shale passed his hand across his head in dazed fashion.

"Nay—nay, Peter," he muttered. "But—but who is this man—what—what does he want?"

Peter swore deeply.

"Zookers, m'lord, methinks 'tis another dastardly attempt upon your life."

Shale smiled grimly.

"Faith, Peter, you become more observant with each passing day," he sighed. "Ah, well, if the fellow meant to kill me, he well nigh succeeded. Turn him over, and let us have a look at him."

At this moment the crowd of guests rushed up excitedly, led by Sir Rupert.

"Gad, m'lord, has the fellow hurt you?" he called.

Shale shook his head.

"Nay, friends, I'm safe enough. But 'tis most unpleasant to know that a man such as this poor fool hath designs upon my life. This day seems bent on being a fateful one in my calendar. Twice have I escaped death by a hair's-breadth."

Lady Genevieve, whose aged feet were not as fleet as those of the younger members of the party, ran panting up and pushed through the circle round Shale and Gloria.

"Geoffrey—Geoffrey," she gasped, throwing her arms about his neck. "I—I thought you were dead by now."

Shale looked vastly embarrassed by her vigorous hugging, and as soon as he could contrive it he slipped from her grasp.

"Zooks, m'lady—I mean aunt—dear—what think you I am—still a toddler at school, eh? In truth, you do most successfully embarrass me—though withal 'tis most pleasant."

Gloria laughed.

"Ah, Geoffrey, you run a mighty risk in giving vent to such delicious compliments. I'm sure if you are not careful Aunt Genevieve will kiss you again."

"Nay, aunt, I beg of you," he pleaded, as she swayed towards him once more. "In private an' you will, but consider that I am a poor man, and my nature makes me feel most foolish to be petted afore company."

"G-g-gad! you're lucky," stammered Sir Brian, gallantly. "I only w-w-wish s-somebody would attempt to s-s-stab m-me."

"Brian," said a firm female voice, "some day you may have your wish if you carry on like that."

Sir Brian caught his wife's baneful glance upon him and, shriveling up completely, he faded back amongst the crowd.

But now the figure of the man lying upon the ground was no longer prostrate.

His fingers moved, then his head and finally he struggled weakly up, upon his hands and knees.

Finally he staggered to his feet, and stood gasping for breath, with hanging head, beside Peter, who watched him narrowly for any signs of returning hostility.

Shale looked at him with elevated brows, then bent forward and gazed into his face.

The man lifted his head and glared fiercely back at him, and his eyes blazed with hatred.

Now seeing this, Shale's face went very pale, and a dull dazed look crept into his eyes.

He gazed around the company slowly, his glance passing from one to the other in a semicircle till it fell upon the Lady Gloria. It lingered there for a moment, then faltered and fell.

"Aye, mine host—and—and to what do I owe the somewhat doubtful pleasure o' this visit o' yours?"

The man glared at him so fiercely that Peter laid a firm hand upon his arm. He shook it off roughly and, with a low growl, spoke.

"Ah, M'lord Anderley, so you know me, eh?"

Shale bowed.

"I do. Are you not Joe Watkins, the landlord of 'Ye Whyte Hart'?"

"I am—and 'tis well that you remember me, for never more will you forget me."

Shale smiled grimly.

"Faith, I hope you're wrong, man, for you have not an overpleasant countenance."

Watkins made a fierce movement of disdain with his arm.

"Scoff—scoff at me, m'lord, 'tis all that you can do, for you know full well why I have come here to you this day looking for your life's blood."

Shale swallowed something in his throat.

He looked on Gloria once more, then he looked on Peter—then on the Lady Genevieve—then once more turned his eyes to the bloody face of the landlord of "Ye Whyte Hart." His voice was harsh when he spoke.

"Well, go on, man—go on."

Watkins grinned wickedly, and rubbed his fat hands.

"Ah, yes, you know full well, m'lord, for was not my pretty Betty in your service at the Hall when last you came home from France?"

Shale gazed steadily at him.

"Well," he said again in a very low voice. "Go on—go on."

With a sudden jerk Watkins freed himself from Peter's grasp and turned furiously to the crowd of extravagantly attired men and women who watched with breathless interest the strange scene.

He lifted up his hand and pointed an accusing finger at Shale.

"There stands the man who stole my Betty— a sweet little innocent daughter—from her father's heart."

The words rang out fierce and loud.

Something like a gasp came from the Lady Gloria—a low sobbing gasp of despair.

Peter emitted a deep growl, and his great fist was raised to strike. Shale looked at him dully and shook his head.

"Nay, nay, Peter. Let him speak—let him speak. Well, man, go on—go on."

Watkins turned, with the hatred still gleaming in his eyes.

"Deny it an' you can," he cried. "You know it's true. She told me so with her own lips before"—his voice broke—"before I put her from my house forever. You ruined my own sweet Betty, you—you——"

He broke off with a deep growl of mingled fierceness and pain.

Then suddenly he sank down upon the ground and burying his face in his great red hands, burst into a fit of sobbing.

"My Betty," he moaned. "Where are you now —where are you now?"

Gloria, with deep pity in her face, knelt beside

him and laid her hand gently upon his shoulder.

"Nay, cry not, poor fellow," she said, "we—we shall find your daughter and bring her back to —to you."

He moaned his sobs out into the air, and slowly Gloria's eyes raised themselves and looked at Shale.

His face was white as death.

"Tell me," she said, "tell me, is—is this true?"

Shale opened his lips to speak, but he uttered no sound and, after gazing dully down at her, he closed them again.

She sprang to her feet, her eyes blazing, and went right up to him.

Still he stood silent as a statue.

She seized his coat by the lapels.

"Speak," she cried fiercely. "Speak—tell me if this is true?"

He gave a deep, deep sigh, and turned away his head.

"Nay, nay, m'lady, do not ask me to speak."

She stood gazing into his face for a full minute and, as she did so, a look of horror came slowly into her countenance.

"Then 'tis true?" she moaned.

Still he stood silent.

"Can you deny it," she went on desperately. "Please—please can you deny it?"

He gently laid his hands on hers and put them down.

Then he stepped back a pace and drew a deep breath.

"M'lady Gloria—M'lady Genevieve—my friends that were, I pray you excuse me. I would take my leave of you."

Lady Genevieve stepped forward.

"Nay, Geoffrey, nay. First you must tell us if this man speaks the truth."

A growl came from Watkins.

"Aye, ask him to speak the truth, m'lady, not I. My words were plain, my conscience clear. I say Lord Anderley stole my daughter from my heart, and well he knows that these words are true."

Shale took two steps forward, but again Lady Genevieve stayed him.

"Tell us, Geoffrey, does—does he speak the truth?"

He bowed his head.

"Aye, m'lady," he said gravely, "to the best of my knowledge, he speaks the truth."

Lady Gloria swayed as if to fall, and he reached out his hand quickly to save her, but with a sweep of her arm she threw it off.

"Touch me not—touch me not, Lord Anderley.

Too much has your presence debased me already."

The deep color flooded his cheeks, then went as quickly as it had come, leaving him pale as the paleness of death.

A shudder seemed to pass through his frame.

"M'lady, m'lady," he whispered brokenly. "It grieves you sore, but—but—ah!—it woundeth me."

He moved again, and they stood silently aside for him to pass.

Even Watkins, fierce-eyed though he was, was powerless of speech, and stared helplessly after him with an uneasy feeling in his heart.

"M'lord, m'lord," cried Peter, running after him. "Where do you go? What do you do?"

He paused and looked at the serving man with tender gaze.

"Ah, Peter, 'tis good of you to ask. I go but back to where I belong, my honest, noble friend."

A look of terror came in Peter's eyes.

"No, m'lord—no," he cried, desperately laying a detaining hand upon his arm. "Nay, not that. Consider what you do. The Lady Gloria, consider her."

Shale looked at him kindly, yet sorrowfully.

" 'Tis for her sake that I go," he said, simply. "For there is nought else to be done, and in very truth 'twas God himself sent Joe Watkins here this day."

"How so, master," asked Peter, dully.

"Because, Peter, his coming saved me from my passion. This moment I am a man, yet a few minutes a-gone I was in the act of deceiving most brutally she for whom I would sacrifice my life —nay, more—my very happiness."

"You mean—m'lord."

"Aye, I mean, Peter, that I might have bartered manhood for love and asked her to wed me, knowing—knowing that I am not what I pretend to be."

He turned and silently resumed his slow, steady walk towards the house.

Amid absolute silence the guests of Sir Humphrey Clayville watched his big broad figure pass round into the stable yard.

A few minutes later there was the sound of hoofs on cobble stones, and a dapple-gray horse cantered down the drive.

On its back was a man with his left arm in a sling, and his head leaning forward upon his breast.

PETER SOBS

THE night shadows were upon Anderley Hall. The birds had ceased them to sing and were gone to rest.

The stillness of the dark was upon the place.

Within a chamber which had been m'lord's sat a man upon the edge of the great four-poster bed.

He was roughly clad, but there was none to note the incongruity of it for the door was closed.

Moreover, it was locked. It had been locked for hours.

Shale sat with his elbows on his knees and his head resting on his hands.

He had not moved from that position since he entered the room. Several times there had been knocks upon the door, but he either had not heard them or had not heeded them.

Now again there was a knock. This time it was a loud knock—a persistent knock that refused to be ignored.

After about two minutes it seemed to convey

its noisy message to his dulled brain, for with a start he sat up.

He looked out through the casement in surprise.

"Dark already," he muttered. "Strange, 'tis dark so soon."

Again that persistent knock—knock—knock.

He rose wearily and crossing turned the key, and jerked the door open.

"Well," he demanded, gruffly.

"Master," said a voice, a deep but hoarse sounding voice. "Master, 'tis I."

Shale breathed deep.

"Aye, Peter, come in, man, come in."

The serving man entered, and silently closed the door behind him.

He crossed over to the table and set the candle he carried down upon it. Turning, he looked at Shale.

"M'lord."

"Nay, Peter. Not m'lord now, man. Call me what you will, but not that."

Peter swallowed a big lump that had arisen in his throat.

"Then, master, it shall be," he said.

Shale shook his head wearily.

"Well, Peter, what want you?"

"To learn where you go, and what you would have me do, master?"

"I go back to the highway, Peter. Back to the hedgerow and the dusty white road. Back to the byways and the wooded paths, Peter. Mayhap to finish my journey to London. Mayhap to wander still further afield."

"But what are you going to do, m'lord?"

"Forget, Peter, or try to forget rather, for I sadly fear that entire forgetfulness is not possible."

"And what am I to do, master?"

"You must stay here, Peter. There is work for you here."

"Work for me, master. Tell me what is it?"

"There are many things that you must do, Peter, and 'tis for that reason that I have awaited your coming."

"Awaited my coming, master. Why I followed you from Clayville Grange immediately, and I have knocked upon your door many times already."

"Faith, that is strange, Peter. I've been here all the while, yet, in sooth, I heard you not."

The tears started to Peter's eyes.

"Master—master—wilt let me follow you and serve you always, and share with you your burdens?"

"Nay, Peter, man. My shoulders are broad enough, though, faith, they've a greater stoop upon them than they had yestere'en. You need have no fear for me. Besides I tell you, man, I have work for you to do here. Wilt perform it for me?"

"Aye, master. You have but to speak, and I will do your bidding ever."

"Then harkee, Peter, to what I say. When I have gone, you must go to where you placed the poor body of Lord Anderley and carry it back to the spot where first we found it."

"But, m'lord, why do that?"

" 'Tis a most cunning way I have schemed me out of accomplishing my disappearance without arousing curiosity, Peter, for if the body of Lord Anderley is found, then will they think that I am dead, and so permit me go my way in peace."

Peter nodded.

"Aye, master. Now I follow your bent."

"Good," said Shale. "Then when they have found the—the body—do you betake yourself to the 'Whyte Hart' and tell Joe Watkins of the violent nature of my death—that his wrath may be appeased and so permit forgiveness for his daughter to enter into his heart."

"Aye, master. What then?"

"Then will you institute thorough search for

poor Betty Watkins, and if she is found—pray
God she be still alive—see that she lacks not for
anything, and when you think fit, reunite her
to her poor father. Such money as you may
spend, and which I now give you, is not mine,
but God knows it will be spent to undo some of
the harm its real owner hath brought about."

There was a long pause.

"Is there aught else, master?"

"Nay, unless it be to persuade Lady Genevieve
to provide a cottage for young Tom Brown, the
stable hand, when he takes pretty Polly Marrow, the smith's daughter, for his wife."

"Aye, master."

Shale looked around the room.

"Dost want anything, master?" queried Peter.

"I was looking for my hat, Peter. A tall,
furry hat it was. Ah, I remember me where it
hath gone."

"Where, master?"

There was a silence. Then, "She hath it, Peter.
Aye, man, there's just one other thing. Wilt tell
her it was my own, and perchance if 'ere she doth
forgive me she may find it in her heart to treasure it."

He took Peter's hand in both of his.

"Peter, man," he said, "I must bid you now
farewell."

A sob broke from the serving man.

"Master, master, my heart goes with you."

He fell upon his knees and pressed his rough lips upon Shale's hands.

They remained thus for a while. Then Shale slowly moved towards the door. With his hand on the handle he turned.

"Peter, my true friend. It hath been good to know you."

Peter raised his eyes like a great faithful dog.

"M'lord, m'lord," he whispered in quivering tones. "Thou are indeed a very lord."

The door swung silently open.

A soft, steady tread sounded a-down the corridor, and faded far away into the distance.

And Peter still knelt upon the floor.

SIR HUMPHREY PERFORMS A PLEASING TASK

'TWAS three days after John Shale's dramatic departure from Clayville Grange.

Lady Gloria had fought against herself during the whole of that time, and never once had she mentioned his name.

Now, rather pale, she sat alone, very, very quietly, in the beauitful drawing room, embroidering a piece of linen.

Sir Humphrey's guests had not departed. They were, in fact, even now out hunting, and she had believed that her uncle had gone with them.

She received an unpleasant shock, however, when she heard his familiar heavy stamping feet in the hall outside, and, looking up quickly, saw his great flabby figure framed in the doorway.

His face was flushed as if he had been drinking, but that was such a usual thing that she almost failed to notice it.

"You're mighty quiet," he said, with something like a sneer.

She bent to her work.

" 'Tis every one's privilege to be quiet when one chooseth," she replied.

He frowned.

"Humph!   Brooding over young Anderley, eh?"

The color deepened in her cheeks, but she did not deign to answer him.

"Well," he said. "Why don't you speak? Art heartbroken because you spurned Lord Anderley and spoiled your chances o' wedding with him?"

Her face went pale again.

"I presume 'tis of small importance to you, Uncle Humphrey, as to whom I wed," she answered, bending down over her embroidery again.

He frowned heavily at her words.

"Well, Gloria," he said gruffly, "you know that your father left you his heritage on condition that you married Lord Anderley."

"Aye," in a low voice. "What has that to do with it, uncle?"

Sir Humphrey turned away to conceal the expression of smug satisfaction on his face.

"Well, Gloria, you ought to know. Did you not send Lord Anderley himself from you in a veritable huff?"

"He left me, uncle, because he knew he could

not look me in the face," she replied, almost in a whisper.

Sir Humphrey rubbed his hands sleepily together.

"Gad! 'twas the least he could do, Gloria. 'Twas doubtless to display what remaining semblance of manhood he might possess."

There was a long silence, broken only by a stifled sob from her ladyship.

"Well, uncle, and what hath that to do with mine heritage?"

He swung round slowly.

"You know full well, Gloria," he said gruffly.

"Nay, uncle, I confess I cannot think what you mean."

He swore deeply, regardless of her presence, as was his wont.

"Egad, Gloria, there's but little use pretending ignorance as to the terms of your father's will. You remember full well that should you fail to wed Lord Anderley your heritage passeth to myself—though I want it but little."

The Lady Gloria drew a deep breath.

"And—and so it is as I had feared, Sir Humphrey," she said. "You intend to press your claim to my estates?"

He walked towards the window of the drawing room wherein they were ere answering.

" 'Tis not my desire to press my claim ere it is justified, Gloria," he said at last. "But as I am sure you will never wed Lord Anderley, there is little use in me withholding from you the fact that I shall become the real heir to Clayville Grange."

He swelled his bosom with pride in such fashion as to bring a smile of scorn to Gloria's lips.

"Methinks you are somewhat in advance of affairs, Sir Humphrey," she replied stiffly, though her face was very white. " 'Twould have been more in keeping with things had you waited till there was not the slightest possibility of my wedding Lord Anderley ere you put forth your claim upon my heritage."

Sir Humphrey swung round with a triumphant gleam in his eyes.

"And is there any chance that I may be thwarted in my desires?" he growled, showing his yellow teeth like a wolf about to spring upon its prey.

She shuddered.

"Perchance I might yet wed Lord Anderley rather than let you enter into the possession of my estates," she said, speaking very softly.

He grinned.

"You are indeed a spiteful miss, m'lady. But, faith, you have still a lot to learn, for let me tell you now that, e'en though you were willing to sink upon your knees and beg of Lord Anderley to take you for his bride, yet he would not wed you."

She looked at him in sudden affright.

"What mean you? An' I asked him, and were willing to forget the—the affair o' the innkeeper's daughter, there's little doubt he would ask me to become his bride."

Sir Humphrey frowned.

"He, he!—but you are surely an uninformed miss," he chuckled. "Hast not heard the news?"

She sat up suddenly.

"The news?" she repeated anxiously. "What news, sir? Tell me, what mean you?"

Again his raucous laugh rang out.

"Gad! I thought every one 'twixt here and London knew it," he said.

She rose to her feet unsteadily, and looked full at him.

"Well, Sir Humphrey, what news? Speak!"

The smile faded from his face, and its place was taken by an ugly sneer. He looked about him, then leaned forward.

"Hast not heard that—that——"

"Well, uncle, well?"

The sneer became more pronounced, and there

was a fierce diabolical ring in his voice when he
spoke.

"That M'lord Anderley is no more," he ground
out.

She swayed as if she would fall, then steadied
herself by clutching hold of the edge of a small
occasional table.

"You mean," she whispered in tense voice.
"You mean—ah!"

He stood back, well pleased with the effect his
announcement was producing.

"I mean what I say, m'lady. Anderley is dead
—dead!"

She stared at him for a long time, as if she
had not heard.

"Dead!" she echoed. "Did'st say he was—was
—dead?"

Sir Humphrey bowed triumphantly.

"Aye, m'lady. I said dead. Gad help us, what's
the matter, Gloria?"

She had suddenly crumpled up, and slid softly
to the floor, there to lie in a faint.

He bent over her for an instant, somewhat
scared at the effect his pronouncement had had;
then, with an oath, he started to his feet and, running to the door, called loudly for assistance.

By the time two maids had arrived on the

scene, however, Gloria's eyes opened and she was struggling to her feet.

They assisted her to a couch and plied her with smelling salts, but she pushed them aside with a sweep of her arm and stared at Sir Humphrey.

"Tell—tell me," she murmured. "What do you mean? Is he really——?"

Her tongue clove to the roof of her mouth and she found she could not speak the dread word.

Sir Humphrey nodded grimly.

"Aye, m'lady, he's dead right enough. There's no doubting it, for his body lies at Anderley Hall this very minute."

She closed her eyes, and her head went back as if in dire pain; then slowly she opened them again.

Now her little white hands were clenched, and a deep, red, hectic spot burned in each of her cheeks.

She rose to her feet unsteadily.

"Give—give order for my chaise to be prepared," she commanded, "and to await me at the front entrance."

Sir Humphrey looked at her.

"Where do you go, Gloria?"

She raised her head.

"I go to—to Anderley Hall, to see him who

was its master," she whispered.

There was a pause.

"Do you doubt my word, m'lady?" growled
Sir Humphrey. " 'Tis the truth I have told you;
I got it by special courier but a few minutes
since."

She shook her head wearily.

"Nay, uncle, I do not doubt you. I would
but look upon his—face—once again, even in
death."

He stared at her till his gaze suddenly faltered.
Then he stood aside as she moved towards the
door, and silently watched her pass from the
room.

When she had gone, a deep malicious scowl
overspread his fat features.

Somehow or other the telling of Lord Anderley's death had not given him the satisfaction he
had thought it would. Realizing this, black fury
seized him, and he lifted up his voice.

"Saddle my horse," he bellowed. "Blast you
all. D'ye hear me? Fetch my nag, and look to
it on the instant. I also hie me to the Anderley
Hall to look upon the dead face of its accursed
master."

DISCLOSES AN INCREDIBLE STATE OF AFFAIRS

WITH a rumbling roar the two-horse chaise which bore the Lady Gloria from Clayville Grange rattled through the gates of Anderley Hall and charged swiftly up the drive, crunching and churning the gravel with hoof and wheel.

The old gateman stood with bared and bowed head as it passed, not even raising his eyes to watch it round the bend to the steps of the house.

The place seemed very silent, and its silence was accentuated by the dull gray clouds that hovered low in the skies. The shutters had all been fastened, and an air of dreary desolation was about the Manor.

Close by the great steps leading to the massive front door stood a horse munching peacefully the sweet, short grass of the well-kept lawn.

It was Sir Humphrey Clayville's.

The chaise slowed up, and finished the last few yards at a slow walk, as if it were doing reverence to the dead.

Then it drew up, and, while the postillion held

237

tight rein upon the champing, prancing horses, the footman leapt to the ground and threw open the door of the carriage.

The Lady Gloria stepped slowly to the ground.

She stood for a moment, as if to steady herself, then softly ascended the steps to the massive door, alone.

All the way from the Grange her heart had been fighting against her mind.

It could not be true, she told herself. It seemed too unreal. She could scarce believe it. But the great, beautiful building, now so somber and formidable with its shuttered casements, drove the dread awfulness of grim reality home to her. There was no gainsaying it. It brazened forth its message of grief as surely as if it had been shouted by heralds from the housetops.

As she neared the door it silently swung open and a slender figure clad in black could be seen standing in the dimness within.

Gloria ran swiftly forward, and clasped the Lady Genevieve in her arms.

For a moment the two women stood thus, sobbing silently. Then Gloria stood back.

"Where—where is—he?" she whispered softly.

Lady Genevieve pointed to the curtained door of the study.

"He—he lies in there, just as we found him."

There was a long pause. Then: "Tell me, dear aunt, how did—it happen?"

Lady Genevieve shook her head.

"I cannot tell. All we know is that he—he was—murdered."

Gloria started back, and her hand went to her lips to stifle the cry of horror that broke from her.

"Aunt—Aunt Genevieve, don't—don't—" she gasped.

The old woman put her arm about her, and led her quietly into the lounge. There, near the window, stood Sir Humphrey Clayville, speaking to Peter and a stable hand. Looking closer, Gloria saw that the latter was Tom Brown, the man who had found the tall, furry hat at Riverhead. The thought flashed through her mind for an instant, then was gone.

Sir Humphrey turned as the women entered. He contrived to conceal the sense of satisfaction that thrilled him. At the same time there seemed a certain uneasiness about him, and his little eyes leaped restlessly to and fro. They were always more or less shifty, but now they seemed shiftier than ever before.

"Well, Gloria, so you've arrived at last. You'd have been better to have stayed at the Grange. This is no work for women. Lord Anderley

has met his death 'at the hands of a foul murderer."

Gloria looked straight at him, but his ever
moving eyes refused to meet hers, and at last
she turned away.

"Where—where was he found?" she asked, in
a low voice.

Tom Brown stepped forward, pulling his forelock awkwardly.

"'Twas I who found him, m'lady. I was
a-walking out my girl, Polly—I mean we was
'aving of a stroll last night, m'lady, and we went
to a place we 'aven't been near for over a week—
the place where I told you, m'lady, as how I'd
seen a hawful happarition, a gloomy gobling it
were, m'lady."

"Yes—yes," breathed Gloria. "Go on—go on."

"Well, m'lady, right where I found that there
queer furry hat which I guv to you that morn
you afired peas at me bandage, ma'am, and
hurted me most sore—an I may say so, m'lady—
well, right on that self-same spot, just where
that gobling was a performing of his spookie
antics, there I found the pore dead body of M'lord
Anderley. God rest his soul."

"Amen," said Peter, fervently.

There was another silence, during which Tom
Brown shuffled uneasily, and Sir Humphrey plied

himself with great quantities of snuff. Then Gloria spoke again:

"Was he badly injured?"

Tom nodded grimly.

"Most horful, m'lady. His face was all a-covered of clotted blood and bashed something fearsome, and there was a bullet hole in his 'ead. 'Tis my belief, m'lady, as how he was shot and then dragged to the spot where I found him, 'cos there was marks on the ground which must 'ave been made by 'is pore corpse."

Gloria shuddered violently, and Lady Genevieve burst into tears. When she had calmed the old woman a little, Gloria spoke again, this time quite calmly.

"Will you please take me to see—him?" she asked, almost in a whisper.

Without answering, Lady Genevieve led the way across the hall to the curtained door of the study and pushed it open.

The place was very dark, save for a few streaks of light which found their way through the chinks of the shutters, and these fell upon something white on the table.

It was a sheet, and it covered a grimly silent form.

Gloria swayed as if to fall; then she felt a strong arm take hers, and, looking up, she saw

Peter staring down at her with a strange look in his eyes.

Somehow or other they seemed to reassure her, and she went forward quite steadily.

Peter slowly drew the sheet down from the poor mutilated face. Gloria stared at it as if fascinated. 'Twas strange she felt no thrill—no terror—no pain, only a dull, ceaseless throb-throb in her brain.

Was this the face she had looked upon with eyes of love. These bloody, battered features were the same. That crisp, curly, black hair was the same. That grim mouth was the same. That chin—that chin—it did not seem so strong somehow, not so firm—yet it, too, was the same.

A low moan of anguish broke from her, and Peter made as if to replace the cover.

As he did so, however, the edge caught in something, and just as he laid it gently down the whole of the sheet slid softly to the floor.

Peter stooped to pick it up again, when suddenly a stifled shriek broke from Gloria, and she clutched at his shoulder for support.

"What's the matter, m'lady?" he gasped, straightening up at once.

"What's wrong, Gloria?" growled out Sir Humphrey.

She raised her right hand and pointed with

quivering finger at the body of Lord Anderley lying on the table.

He was clad in shirt, knee breeches and riding boots. His sleeves were torn, and his arms lay spread out upon the table.

Gloria was staring at him with dead-white face and glowing eyes.

"That—that is not Lord Anderley!"

Lady Genevieve gave a little scream. Sir Humphrey swore. Peter turned his eyes away and his fingers twitched.

"What mean you?" demanded Sir Humphrey gruffly. "Are you mad, girl?"

She passed her hand across her head in dreary fashion.

"I—I must be—yet look!—look!—where is the deep sword-wound on his left arm, which I myself bound up after he fought the duel—with Aylesbury?"

Sir Humphrey stared, then gasped and gulped. Lady Genevieve rubbed her eyes incredulously, and Peter muttered "Zookers" beneath his breath.

At last Sir Humphrey spoke.

"By gad, the wound has gone." He looked closer. "There has never been any wound there, 'tis absolutely unscarred."

Suddenly he swung round and caught Peter's eyes upon him with a strange, baneful glare.

He looked again at the dead man, then a great shiver shook his flabby frame. When he raised his face, all saw that it was ghastly pale.

Peter spread the sheet over his dead master's body, and silently they filed from the room.

THE SMITH AT RIVERHEAD BRINGS STARTLING
NEWS

IN the lounge they stood staring one at the other in dull perplexity.

Peter alone seemed to be unaffected by the strange air of mystery which was rapidly making its presence felt.

" 'Tis mighty queer," muttered Sir Humphrey, striding back and forward with his hands behind his back, in pondering mood.

Neither of the women spoke. The whole thing seemed beyond them. It was too impossible to imagine that there should be no trace of that wound in Lord Anderley's arm after so short a lapse of time, yet undoubtedly this was the case.

Suddenly Gloria spoke in a firm voice.

"If that man was Lord Anderley, there would have been a mark of the wound upon his arm."

Lady Genevieve drew a deep breath, and shook her head.

"Nay, child—no matter what you say, that is Lord Anderley. Have I not known him all my life? Have I not dangled him upon my knee?"

She turned to Peter.

"Have you any doubts, Peter?"

He shook his head slowly.

"Nay, m'lady, 'tis Lord Anderley sure enough. An' you doubt it, 'tis easily proved."

"How?" demanded Sir Humphrey.

"By the birthmark m'lord bore upon his right shoulder, sir."

Lady Genevieve started.

"Yes, yes," she cried excitedly, " 'twas a large mole the size of a crown. I remember it full well when he was but a babe."

Sir Humphrey strode heavily from the room. They heard him cross the hall and enter the other room.

Breathlessly the women awaited his return. Peter crossed to the window and stood silently gazing out.

Sir Humphrey's bespurred boots sounded in the hall again, and they all looked at him.

He grunted.

"Right enough," he said. "The mark's there full plain. I'faith, 'tis queer."

Silence fell again, then of a sudden the distant sound of galloping hoofs was borne in upon them.

Nearer they came and nearer till now they sounded close outside.

Then with a grinding clatter they came to a halt.

Peter, at the window, gave a gasp of surprise.

"What is it, man?" cried Sir Humphrey, coming to his side.

He looked through the half-closed shutters.

"Gad, 'tis the smith of Riverhead—big Jem Marrow, an' I'm a knight. What wants he here?"

There was the sound of noisy knocking on the outer door, and Peter hastened to admit the man.

"I want M'lady Collingway," he gasped. "Take me to her quick. I have news of first import."

Peter led him into the lounge and there he stood bowing and scraping before the gentry.

He was a strange figure in that luxurious room. Still clad in shirt and leathern apron—hatless and streaming with perspiration—'twas plain that he had come post-haste to the Hall to impart his tidings whate'er they were.

"Well, man," growled Sir Humphrey. "What is it? Speak."

"M'ladies, Sire, I have strange news to tell— news I can scarce myself understand."

"Well, well," broke in Sir Humphrey, impatiently, "get on with it, knave."

Big Jem Marrow drew a deep breath, then burst out——

"I have seen Lord Anderley near the village."

Had a thunderbolt fallen from the skies at their feet it could not have struck more amazement into the hearts of his hearers.

Sir Humphrey recovered his senses first and seized the smith by his shoulder.

"What, man!" he roared. "Do you try to play a trick upon us."

Jem Marrow pushed him gently but firmly back.

"Nay, master. I speak the truth. But an hour since I was gathering kindling wood for my forge some little distance down from Riverhead and in so doing I chanced to wander me further into the forest than I had intended. And coming suddenly into a green glade I started back in affright, for there asleep upon the grass lay a man. And as I looked at him I could scarce believe my own eyes, for, an' I be struck dead this instant, I was staring at the face of Lord Anderley."

Sir Humphrey and the two women stared at him in amaze. Peter alone stood calm and unperturbed.

"I thought at first I was seeing a ghost," went on the smith, "but as I looked I knew I was gazing at a living man, for even as I stared he yawned and stretched his limbs. Then did I draw back into the woods and watch him arise to his feet. But still was I sorely affrighted, so that when he walked away into the forest whistling right merrily I did not have me the heart to follow him, but stood hidden and dazedlike watching him till he passed out of sight, which was mighty quick, for the woods are thick thereabouts. Then did I go home and thereafter ride here posthaste."

Sir Humphrey looked at him keenly.

"You're sure you made no mistake."

The smith shook his head vigorously.

"Nay, master. I know m'lord's face. Did I not carry him to the Hall last night when we found his body."

Suddenly Gloria spoke.

"Did you notice anything else—anything strange about his left arm?"

The smith scratched his white-haired head.

"Now as you mention it, m'lady, when he arose his arm seemed to pain him somewhat and he cried aloud, 'May Aylesbury's cursed sword be damned.'"

A startled exclamation broke from Gloria, but Sir Humphrey stayed her when she would have questioned the smith further.

"Was there aught else, smith," he asked, gruffly.

"Nay, master," replied the man. "That was all I saw, and I thought it of such import that I came to the Hall at once."

After a moment's pause, Sir Humphrey tossed the man a coin.

"That for your pains," he said, gruffly. "And, mark you, you keep your mouth tight shut on this matter in the village."

Jem touched his white forelock and, turning, walked with stately mien from the room.

When he had gone, Sir Humphrey emitted a string of oaths.

"'Tis plain we have been tricked," he said.

"What mean you?" asked Lady Genevieve.

He swung round fiercely.

"I mean that the man who left us three days since was the man whom the smith saw this morning."

Gloria rose wearily.

"His left arm pained him," she muttered. "'Twas he."

"Aye," scowled Sir Humphrey. "'Twas he. But that's not all. 'Tis just as plain that he was not Lord Anderley."

There was a profound silence.

"You—you mean?" gasped Lady Genevieve at last. "That he was an impostor."

Sir Humphrey nodded.

"Thou hast said it, Lady Genevieve. He was an impostor, a damnable roguish adventurer."

Gloria turned away to hide her face.

Lady Genevieve rose unsteadily to her feet.

"I—I thought there was something different about—the man who—who came back from France. He did not seem the same as poor Geoffrey somehow, and now when I think of it there were many things he did which showed that he was not familiar with the place as Geoffrey had been. Then, too, there was the wonderful way he fenced and besides he seemed bigger and broader and stronger-willed and somehow—more —more—as I would have had my boy be."

She buried her face in her hands and burst into a storm of hysterical weeping.

Gloria tried to calm and soothe her, and in a few minutes she had persuaded her to go to her room and lie down. Sir Humphrey seized the opportunity to depart also.

When she had gone, the girl turned to Peter, who seemed to be trying to slip out of the room.

"Where are you going?"

He stopped and looked at her awkwardly.

"I'm j—just going to—to——"

"Yes, Peter?"

"To Sevenoaks, m'lady."

"Why, Peter?"

He shuffled his feet.

"Tell me, Peter," she pressed.

"Well, m'lady, I just thought as how it would be well to—to tell old Joe Watkins, of the 'Whyte Hart,' that m'lord is dead. It might ease his mind somewhat, m'lady."

She turned away.

As Peter looked at her he thought somehow that she did not seem so sadlike as before. Did her eyes actually have a gleam of brightness in them, or was he mistaken?

"Yes, Peter," she said at last. " 'Twere a charitable thing to do—but 'tis work more suited for a woman than a man, so I will drive me to Sevenoaks with you."

Peter stared, then gulped down a lump in his throat.

"Zookers, m'lady. But you're just as good and kind as—as he was, m'lady."

Now as the serving man stared he saw a great pearl-like tear trickle gently down the pale cheek.

"And yet, Peter," she whispered "he—he was but an impostor."

Peter bowed his head upon his breast as though the thought brought him profound pain.

"Nay, nay, m'lady," his hoarse voice sounded. "He is in truth a very man—a very man."

She raised her face.

"Peter, did'st say he 'is'? Do I hear aright?"

"Aye, m'lady, I said 'is,' for I pray God he still lives."

Now a new light came into m'lady's eyes, and the rich red blood crept once more into her sweet face.

"Let us go," she said.

SHOWS PETER IN A VINDICTIVE MOOD

A SUDDEN silence fell upon the farm hands who loafed round the bar of the taproom of "Ye Olde Whyte Hart," and all eyes were turned towards the door.

Only a moment before, laughter and jovial voices had rung high, yet now you could have heard a pin drop.

Gentlefolks had arrived at the inn. Through the narrow window-panes the loiterers could see a chaise drawn up by the roadside. And now its occupants were within the great rough taproom.

One of them was a girl, and the other was a man.

She was slim, graceful, sweet-faced, tiny footed, daintily clad with entrancing ringlets of golden hair dangling beneath her beflowered bonnet. She stopped just inside the door and dropped a dainty curtsey that sent the hands of the men quickly to their heads to tug off their coarse caps, the while they stood gaping and ill at ease before her.

The man who followed her was a tall fellow, big of bone and with rough brown face. He was coarsely clad, and even those ignorant yokels knew that he was not of the quality.

Joe Watkins hastily dropped the beer mug he was filling and, drying his hands upon his apron, ran excitedly around the bar to receive the visitors.

"This way, ma'am," he cried, pointing to a door. "There's a fine parlor here—'tis the best I've got and there's nought but gentry use——"

He stopped suddenly, and remained staring at her face.

Then as he looked the pleasant expression left his own, and its place was taken by an ugly scowl.

"Ah—ah!" he muttered. "So 'tis M'lady Clayville who honors my poor place, is it?"

Gloria raised her head imperiously, and Peter stepped forward with threatening mien.

Her uplifted hand detained him, however, and he hung back.

"Yes, Master Watkins, 'tis the Lady Clayville," she said. "Art not pleased to see me?"

Joe bowed and scraped, but withal it was done with an ill grace, then he turned and led the way to the parlor which had only been used by gentry.

Within it Gloria seated herself on a hard oak chair.

"Well, m'lady, what brings you to honor a poor place like mine," said Watkins.

She looked him over with something like pity. Then she gazed down at her buckled shoe peeping from beneath her dress.

"I was sorry for you, Watkins, when you told us about—about your daughter."

The grimness of the man's face grew more drawn.

"Aye," he muttered. "But I need not your pity."

She frowned.

"Nay, but methinks your daughter does," she said softly.

"Well, what an' she does?"

She looked up at him.

"Have you heard that—that Lord Anderley is dead?"

He nodded grimly.

"Aye. He but saved me the killing of him."

She flushed.

"Do you not know that you are in a peculiar position, Watkins?"

He looked at her suspiciously.

"I be a simple man, m'lady, and am no hand at riddles."

"Well," she went on. "Perhaps you may understand when I tell you that—Lord Anderley was—was foully murdered."

Watkins started.

"What's that you say, ma'am? Murdered! Well, ma'am, what o't?"

She leaned towards him.

"Do you not remember you threatened to kill him three days ago?"

The innkeeper's face went deadly pale. He looked about him like a rat in a trap looking for a loophole of escape. Then he wrung his hands together.

"M'lady! What mean you? Surely you do not think—surely no one thinks that I—that— I——"

He stopped, too terror-stricken to say more.

Gloria rose to her feet.

"Nay, Watkins, I do not think you had aught to do with it, but there's others who may, and for that reason I have come to warn you to be on your guard."

The innkeeper swayed unsteadily.

"M'lady—m'lady, 'tis good of you," he moaned, "but what am I to do. A poor man like me. How can I save myself if they suspect me. Oh, think what would my little Betty do if her father was sent to the gallows an innocent man."

"You did not think of that three days since," said Peter, gruffly. "Where is she now?"

"She is in Sevenoaks with an aunt of hers," whimpered the distracted fellow. "I banished her from my house."

Gloria looked at him.

"If I promise to protect you as much as is in my power, will you promise to forgive her?" she demanded.

Watkins' scowl returned.

"She hath ruined her life, and brought deep disgrace upon my house," he began.

Gloria turned to the door.

"Then if you refuse to forgive her fully and absolutely, I must withdraw my protection from you. Do not forget that my uncle, Sir Humphrey Clayville, is magistrate of this county, and he hath it in his power to hang you or let you live if he pleases."

This set the poor man to shivering again, and to hastily protesting that he meant no harm, and would forgive his daughter freely.

Suddenly he burst into tears.

"In truth, I am but longing to take her to my heart again, for she is my only child and needeth my protection and comfort more than I have given it afore, m'lady," he blubbered.

Gloria soothed him by promising that she

would make sure that he was not suspected of the crime about which she could see he knew nothing.

" 'Twas fortunate for you that you did not succeed in your purpose when you visited the Grange," she said.

"Aye, m'lady," he agreed. " 'Twas fortunate."

"And for more reasons than one," went on Gloria.

"For why, m'lady," he queried, stemming his tears with his apron.

"Because you would have killed the wrong man. The man you attacked was not Lord Anderly."

"Not Lord Anderley, m'lady! But I saw him, and I knew Lord Anderley, because he stopped at my inn on his way home from France—didn't he, friend," he added turning to Peter.

Peter nodded awkwardly, and tried to keep the deep flush from overspreading his features. Things were not shaping quite as he had expected. There was no knowing what this babbling fool might disclose to her ladyship if they remained here longer.

Gloria shook her head.

"Nevertheless, you well nigh killed the wrong man," she said. "For the man you saw was not Lord Anderley, but—but—" her voice dropped

almost to a whisper and quivered sadly, though
she kept on with brave mien, "but—an impostor,"
she concluded with a stifled sob.

"M'lady, think what you say," gasped Peter
in anguish.

She looked at him with tears in her eyes.

"Aye, I think well of what I say, friend Peter,
'tis plain that the countryside will be babbling of
the affair soon enough, and 'tis better that they
should know the truth than invent their own
account."

Peter groaned, but stopped when Joe Watkins
eagerly broke in.

"Ah, m'lady. Do you speak the truth?"

"Without a doubt," she answered in drear
tone.

Joe whistled in amaze.

"Then I know who that man was."

"What man?" she asked quickly.

"Why, the—the impost—the what you called
him, m'lady."

She smiled weakly, but withal there was eager
curiosity in her voice when she spoke.

"You mean the—impostor?" she said.

"That's him," went on the innkeeper. "I know
who he is! Why, 'tis plain as a signpost. I'd
stake my life on it."

"Beware or it mayn't be yours to stake," quoth

Peter furiously, but he shriveled up into silent glowering before her ladyship's eyes.

She turned eagerly to Watkins.

"Well, who do you think this man is?"

The fellow drew a deep breath.

"Why, he's a farmer named Shale—John Shale, and I think he used to farm a place named Dene Farm down Tonbridge way, on one of Sir Humphrey Clayville's estates, but I overheard him tell M'lord Anderley that he was turned out when the lease was up."

Gloria swayed as if to fall, and Peter with a furious glare at Watkins, held out his hand to support her. Her eyes were closed for an instant, but she opened them again at his touch.

"Did—did he meet Lord Anderley here?" she asked.

"Aye, m'lady," replied the man. "On that very night m'lord stopped here. He fought him a duel."

"A duel," gasped Gloria. "Tell me—how was that—what caused it and who—who—won?"

Joe felt his bosom swell with pride at the interest his story was arousing, though withal he could not understand the fierce scowls Peter was casting in his direction.

"Why, 'twas like this, m'lady. M'lord noticin' this farmer Shale's wonderful likeness to

himself, he asked him to sup with him and thereafter proposed a toast to you, m'lady, in which
he recounted certain stories anent you, m'lady—
gossip they was, for which I don't take no account
of, but, m'lord, he told them to this Shale, and
he made so bold, m'lady, as to tell m'lord as how
he shouldn't have so done, and thereupon, m'lady,
Lord Anderley he forced this farmer to cross
swords with him in my taproom, ma'am."

He paused to get breath, then proceeded while
Gloria listened with wide open glowing eyes and
heaving bosom.

"Well, well," she whispered. "Who won, quick,
man, tell me?"

" 'Twas the farmer fellow as won, m'lady,
which was greatly to my surprise, for I thought
m'lord would leave me his dead body on my
hands, but by the grace of God I was spared
bloodshed, for by a trick this Shale he caught
m'lord's sword and held him at his mercy, but he
spared his life, whereupon m'lord paid for all the
suppers and parted with this Shale in most
friendly fashion."

Gloria turned her head that they should not
see the tears glistening in her eyes. He had
fought for her—to shield her name—and he did
not know her, had never seen her, and had no
thought of ever meeting her at the time.

She put her hand into her purse and withdrew a golden guinea which she handed to the innkeeper.

"Just one thing more, Watkins," she said in a very low voice, "should you perchance meet this—this man, Shale, again, what would you do?"

Joe pondered, then spoke.

"Hast never thought that if he took m'lord's place, 'tis more than likely that he killed him first."

A hoarse oath broke from Peter, and his great fist rose to strike.

"Nay, Peter, nay," cried Gloria, and the arm fell to his side again.

Gloria looked at the innkeeper a long time. Her face was white now, and her lips quivered.

"Then—then if you should meet him what would you do?" she asked.

"Faith, m'lady, I think 'twould be safest to let the watch at Sevenoaks know of his presence."

Gloria turned on him furiously.

"So that is how you would treat a man suspected of the crime you yourself might well have been hung for."

Joe stammered and stuttered.

"Nay, m'lady, I had not thought o' that.

'Twould lie with you, m'lady, if you wished——"

She made a gesture commanding silence.

"Should you at any time meet that man, Shale," she ordered imperiously, "see that he has food and shelter, and beware that he comes to no harm through your meeting of him."

She turned swiftly and walked from the room, followed by Peter who, watching his opportunity bestowed a sudden vicious kick upon the innkeeper that brought a yell of pain from his lips.

"And beware you keep your promises," said Lord Anderley's servant grimly—"or by zookers there's more to come."

A minute later the horses snorted, the postillions cracked their whips, hoofs clattered upon cobbles and with a rumbling rattle the chaise swung out into the highway.

APPERTAINS TO THE HAUNTING AND HUNTING OF
A MAN

THE deep darkness of night was upon the
great white road.

The trees stood out like gaunt sentinels against
the starry blackness of the skies.

The moon was on the wane, and its timid light
seemed to fall almost furtively upon the ground.

It attracted no attention to itself, but rather
served only to accentuate the somberness of the
gloom. It cast shadows upon the white way and,
as the thin clouds in the sky drifted across its
light, these shadows disappeared and appeared
again in most disconcerting fashion.

There was no wind to make a stir in the trees
and utter silence prevailed. Not even the cry of
a night hawk broke its dread dreariness—only
the steady measured tramp—tramp—tramp of a
solitary man.

John Shale trudged along the highway, keeping right in its center, and the moon threw his
long shadow many yards ahead of him.

It swayed to and fro most tantalizingly, and

the manner in which it rose and fell upon the humps and hollows of the road gave it a weird grotesqueness that made chill shivers run down the spine of the man, strong willed and fearless though he was.

"Gad, I love the highway, but I love it in the company of humans, not of ghosts—or of gruesome shadows that seem like ghosts," he muttered to himself. "Three whole days and four nights have I hung around this place for no fixed purpose that I can think o'—unless it be to gain just one last glimpse o' her sweet face and perchance to see how she hath taken the news o' my death."

He shuddered at the word, then raised his head quickly at the soft sound of rustling leaves in the wood upon his left.

He stopped and looked towards the spot quickly.

Now in the utter silence which prevailed, the mem'ry of his footsteps seemed like the echoed report o' thunder.

For a full minute he stood thus, then with a jerky laugh he moved forward again.

"Faith, my nerves are running away with me," he said to himself. "Yet I could have sworn I heard a sound of something move over there—

the sound of man or beast or—" Again he shuddered.

He walked a few yards.

Suddenly he stopped.

Once more there was that queer swishing sound amongst the bushes.

Shale felt his hair stiffen. He was a man who knew no fear, but the eerie feeling that wooded roads and utter loneliness inspire in every living soul, gripped him as it would any other.

He clenched his fists and raised his voice.

"Who's there?" he called, his tones booming out into the blackness and passing amongst the trees as they echoed their way to nothingness in a fading repetition of the words—"who's there —who's—there—who's—there—who's—there."

It was like mocking ghostly voices whispering his question one to the other.

Again silence—dead silence.

Shale took two steps forward towards the spot whence the rustle of the leaves had seemed to come, then stopped quickly.

There it was again. "Rustle—rustle—swish— swish."

With a mighty leap, he landed himself at the edge of the roadway and plunged into the bushes.

There was a scurrying scuffle and the crash of a heavy body forcing its way through the bracken.

Shale gave a low cry and dashed in the direction of the sound.

In a few seconds he saw a big round black shape ahead of him, flitting amongst the trees.

With a fierce oath he sprang at it.

'Twas just in front of him now, and with his mighty jump he was upon it and brought it crashing to the ground.

"Be you man or devil," he groaned out hoarsely between his teeth. "I've got you."

A piercing shriek rent the night air, then a terror-stricken voice raised itself hysterically.

"Spare me, spare me, Simon. I've told no one—I've told no one."

Shale dragged the man to his feet, and with hands on the collar of his coat he rushed him through the bushes out into the gloomy light of the moon.

"Spare me, Simon. Don't kill me," whimpered the quaking wretch. "Don't kill me."

Shale swung him round and gazed into his face.

The instant he did so he gave a mighty start, and in sheer amaze released the fellow.

"Gad! it's little Benjamin," he said. "Fat little Benjamin."

Now the man ceased his sniveling and opened his eyes in astonishment.

When they lighted on Shale's face, a look of horror came into them, and with another piercing shriek he turned and fled headlong down the roadway.

"Stop, man, stop," shouted Shale, dashing after him, but the more he called, the harder the little man ran.

Now a regular race ensued, but though terror made Benjamin's feet fairly fly, he was no match for Shale, and the race was but a short one. In a minute he was caught, but still he struggled desperately to get away again.

At last he collapsed on the roadway, shaking like a leaf with fright.

"Spare me, m'lord. Spare me. It was not I—indeed it was not, it—it was Simon—foul, heartless Simon."

Shale looked down at him.

"What mean you, fool? I intend you no harm. Get upon thy feet, and be a man. I would hear what you have to say. Why you have watched me, and why have you called me first Simon, and then m'lord?"

The man rose quivering to his feet.

"I—I tell you, m'lord, it was not I," he began.

Shale dropped an oath.

"Why call me m'lord. I am no lord—I am

but a poor farming fellow with no farm now, alas!—and my name is John Shale."

At his words, the other stopped shaking, and gaped up at him in glad surprise.

A queer little laugh broke from him.

"He-he-he. He-he-he-he-" he giggled delightedly. "John Shale, oh—yes, demme—John Shale—Gad—egad—John Shale."

The other frowned.

"Well," he demanded, impatiently. "What of it? Art madman, or art but a babbling fool. Speak!"

The fellow grinned up at him.

"So you're John Shale, eh," he muttered, "well no wonder you passed as Lord Anderley. You're his very image."

Shale started violently, and seized him by the shoulder.

"What d'ye mean?" he growled fiercely. "Who told you this?"

The impudent grin vanished from the man's face.

"Let me be then, and I may tell you," he said. "Aye, mayhap you'll say yet that you're glad you met me."

Shale released him.

"Go on, then. Tell me what you know or—or," and his voice had an ominous ring in it.

"What I know is not much," said the man. "I know only what the whole countryside will know to-morrow, an' it doesn't know already. But, faith, I can see you don't know it, though it concerns you vastly."

"Speak not in riddles, knave. Quicken thy tongue, or you'll repent it."

"Easy, master, easy. I'm being as smart as a fat man like me can be. All I know is that you posed as Lord Anderley, and—and——"

He glanced furtively around.

"Well, go on—Aye?" put in Shale, impatiently.

The little man looked at him queerly.

"And also, friend, that you are wanted for the"—— a shudder ran through his frame, and his voice dropped to a hoarse whisper—"for the murder of that same Lord Anderley."

Shale stared. Then he pressed his hands dazed-like to his temples.

"For the—murder—of Lord Anderley," he echoed slowly.

"Aye, John Shale," said the little man. "I tell you true—and I tell you but to warn you. 'Forewarned is forearmed,' friend, as I well know. Were I not forewarned of Simon's murderous bent upon my life, I'd be a corpse ere now."

Shale's brain grappled with the problem. He

had never thought of this before, yet now he knew it was an almost natural thing to take place if ever it was revealed that he had posed as the master of Anderley Hall.

And so it must have been revealed. Some one must have found out that he was not the real Lord Anderley and at once the conclusion that he had slain the noble and taken his place, had been jumped to.

"But it is a lie—a vile utter lie," he gasped, fiercely staring down at Benjamin.

The little man nodded his head wisely.

"Aye, 'tis a lie, but nevertheless 'twill be difficult for you to prove it," he said, "and so I would advise you to get you out of Kent at greatest possible speed."

A deep oath broke from Shale. He felt himself being gripped by a mighty wrath.

"How did you learn this," he growled.

" 'Twas simple enough. Outside the gate of Sir Humphrey Clayville's manor—Clayville Grange—a notice hath been erected offering a reward for you—your body, alive or dead. 'Tis signed by Sir Humphrey himself, as district magistrate."

Shale felt his passion rise.

"So he's blazoning it forth throughout the countryside," he hissed. "He—he hath dared

to call me murderer—the man who himself sent
Lord Anderley to his doom."

Benjamin started.

"Who told you that?" he gasped quickly.

Shale looked at him and suddenly recollected
that he was gazing at one of the men whom he
felt convinced had been paid by Sir Humphrey to
do his dirty work.

His hand went out and grabbed the fellow by
the throat.

" 'Twas you and that other rogue, Simon, who
did the foul deed," he roared. "Confess, knave,
confess, or I'll choke the very life from your
carcass."

The other's face blanched.

"Nay—nay, master—'twas not I—do not kill
me—'twas not I."

"Confess, or go to hell with your crime upon
your soul," growled Shale with fierce passion.

" 'Twas not I," screamed the wretch in terror.
"I tell 'ee 'twas not I—'twas Simon Grappletight—I tried to stay him, but he fired ere I
could give warning to m'lord. I swear before
God 'tis truth I speak."

Shale released him, and stood glowering furiously down upon him.

"Ay, so it was Simon, eh?" he hissed. " 'Tis
well you told me, or I would have been a mur-

derer in very truth, and you my victim. But
now you will come with me and tell the world;
'twill never be said that John Shale's name was
blazoned abroad as a wanted man—a hunted
murderer. If they want me they'll get me—aye
—and you'll get the reward, Benjamin. The
hundred guineas will be yours."

The man looked at him in scared perplexity.

"Me get the reward—what mean you, master?"

Shale smiled with ominous grimness.

"I mean that you will accompany me, and
together we'll visit Sir Humphrey Clayville and
tell him who killed Lord Anderley. Aye, you'll
tell them 'twas Simon, and you'll say also who
it was paid him to do it. 'Twill come well from
the lips of you, Benjamin, since you can vouch
for Sir Humphrey's guilt. Then, friend, the
hunter may become the hunted, and you, Benjamin, shall have an easy conscience at last."

Benjamin looked about him in terror.

"No, no, master. Not that. Anything but
that."

Shale looked at him fiercely.

"You'd let me be branded as a murderer, eh?"
he growled. "You foul, cowardly knave."

Benjamin quaked again.

"Oh, what am I to do, master?" he cried in
terror. "Harkee, I would go with you an' I could,

but on the day that I tell the truth of Lord
Anderley's death, Simon Grappletight will stick
a foot of steel into my heart. He hath sworn
to do it. Ah, woe is me."

Shale growled.

"So that's why you were watching me, eh?
You thought I was Simon, and you were awaiting your chance to slay him?"

Benjamin nodded.

"Aye, master—he knows that I am haunted
by the face of the man he shot, and, being afraid
that one day I should betray him, he hath sworn
to kill me."

Shale scowled

"No matter," he said doggedly. "You, and
you alone, can prove my innocence, and so, friend
Benjamin, this night you go with me."

The poor fellow groaned.

"Have mercy on me, man," he pleaded. "Do
you not see that I will be taken as an accomplice
in crime and will be hung for very sure?"

Shale shook his head.

"Nay, friend, an' you speak the truth your
king's evidence will save your well-stretched
skin. Come, let us continue down the highway.
We will hie ourselves to Clayville Grange."

He took the other's arm, and led him, still

protesting vigorously, in the direction of Orpington.

After they had proceeded a few yards Benjamin seemed to become resigned to the turn affairs had taken.

"Release my arm, master. Your fingers bite into my tender flesh. I will accompany you in quietude."

Shale released him, but kept a wary eye upon him as they walked steadily down the dusty road.

"I am indeed a most unlucky wretch," quoth Benjamin, "for, faith, no matter where I turn or what I do, it 'pears to me misfortune stareth me in the face."

" 'Tis thy own fault, man," growled Shale. "But most of all 'tis Sir Humphrey Clayville's. How he hath gotten my name is more than I can tell, but that he should besmirch it with the name o' murder—aye, and murder which his own evil mind did plan—is more than I'll forbear."

He thought of the Lady Gloria. Did she believe this foul slander? Was she, too, aiding in the search? Or did she think of him with thoughts of sorrow and pity?

The blood surged into his brain. He felt his wrath rising till it seemed he must cry aloud in very fierceness.

They reached a bend in the white road. 'Twas very dark here, for the moon was hidden behind a thick cloud. Bushes were at one side of them, cut off from the road by a deep ditch near which Shale walked. At the other side was an open wood, black with trees, but fairly free from underbrush.

Shale swung round the corner. 'Twas then that Benjamin saw his chance, and took it.

With Shale's back towards him for an instant he lowered his head and, like a fierce bull, charged.

There was a crash as his bulky carcass, hurled forward with all the strength of his little fat legs, struck Shale's mighty form.

Taken unawares, the latter staggered and pitched forward.

A fierce oath broke from his lips as he strove to recover. His foot went out like lightning to save himself, but instead of striking firm ground it crashed through a mass of weeds and ferns, and next instant he felt himself falling headlong into the deep ditch.

He landed on his left shoulder and side, and a gasp of pain broke from him as the terrific impact tore open the barely healed wound which Aylesbury's sword had made in his arm.

For a moment he lay dazed; then, with a fierce

yell of black fury, he raised himself to his feet and scrambled out upon the roadway.

He was just in time to catch a glimpse in the darkness of a great figure disappearing amongst the trees at the other side of the road.

Again that awful yell of rage rang out upon the still night air, and, like a bullet from a catapult, the maddened man leapt forward into the wood.

The leaves on the ground scattered hither and thither beneath his flying feet as he plunged through the trees. His threatening shouts echoed across the forest, and smote the ears of Benjamin Greenleaf, so that he was filled with a terrible terror that gave strength to his legs and made him run as he had never run before.

He glanced fearfully behind him and saw that the blackness of the forest made it impossible for him to see his pursuer, or for the latter to see him.

The cunning of a fox was in Benjamin's brain now, and like lightning he darted away to the left.

He paused for an instant and heard the crashing of bushes on his right.

Grim terror told him that the fates were on his side.

Now, like a cat, he turned and crept softly, silently back whence he had come.

At first he went slowly, stopping to listen every minute or so to the hoarse yells of his infuriated pursuer and the crashing of his heavy body through the bushes.

Gradually it seemed to him that the sounds were going away from him. At first 'twas hardly noticeable, but soon the noise got fainter and fainter, until, with a sigh of relief, Benjamin stopped and, seating himself upon a fallen tree, wiped the sweat from his brow and gave thanks to God for a merciful escape.

A hundred yards away John Shale continued his mad career through the woods.

His clothes caught in bushes, tearing them to ribbons. Thorns scratched his face and arms ruthlessly, but he heeded them not. His mighty form crashed young trees to the ground, and trampled tall ferns underfoot. His face was contorted with fury, and with each step the glare in his eyes became more desperate.

He shouted no longer, but saved his breath for the chase.

Now he stopped suddenly, and stood listening.

The dead silence of the night was upon the woods. Not a sound did he hear, not a whisper amongst the trees.

" 'Twas this way the fellow ran, I'll swear me," he muttered. "He's hiding somewhere."

He pressed forward again, and now deep despair settled upon him. He saw his only hope of clearing his name of the foul charge of murder slipping away into the night.

He was a branded murderer, and SHE would know him as such. She would hear of him being hunted and hounded from place to place, from hedge to wood, from tree to tree, till at last they caught him. And then—then she would hear of him being hung upon the scaffold.

The thought brought the black fury upon him again, and with a hoarse cry he plunged forward.

The bushes swayed and fell before him, the ground quivered beneath his heavy tread. Then all at once he saw a flicker of light.

He stopped instantly and stared through the trees.

There it was again. There was no mistaking it—a light flickered bright in the deep darkness of the forest.

He turned fiercely and strode towards it. Had he asked himself why he did so he couldn't have told. Something seemed to lure him forward to that light, as the glare of a candle lures a moth to destruction. He thrust the bushes aside from his path with his hands, and felt not even the pain of his fresh-bleeding wound.

Once he raised his left arm to dash aside the drops of perspiration from his forehead, and his blood drew a long streak of red across his face.

He now came rapidly nearer the light, and suddenly, with a last plunge, he burst out of the forest on to the highway again.

Before him stood a great iron gate. In a hazy sort of way it seemed familiar to him.

On one side of it stood a post stuck deep into the ground, and on the top of this post a lantern was hung.

'Twas this light that had lured Shale from the forest.

He stared at it as if fascinated.

Beneath it was a notice board.

His eyes wandered from the light to the board, and he stood very, very still as he read the words written in red paint thereon.

> 100 Guineas Reward for the Body of John Shale—MURDERER AND IM-POSTOR. Bears striking resemblance to Lord Anderley of Anderley Hall. ALIVE OR DEAD.

For a moment Shale stood staring dumbly at the notice. Then a hoarse cry broke from him, and like a man demented he hurled himself at the post.

There was the sound of a mighty impact— a crack like a pistol shot, as his great, powerful body smote it headlong.

With a splintering crash the signpost swayed, tottered, and then fell.

AN UNEXPECTED VISITOR ARRIVES

WITHIN the great drawing room of Clayville Grange the guests of Sir Humphrey Clayville and his niece, Lady Gloria, laughed and chattered right merrily.

Most of the members of the houseparty were there, and the few who were not were reclining in the ante-room, which was curtained off with a gorgeous blue and gold drapery taking up nearly half of one wall opposite the door.

A log fire was burning in the hearth, but it was rather warm and the long casement, which reached to the floor and opened on to the lawn, was a little ajar.

The women were doing the most of the talking, for the male members of the company looked bored, and some yawned unrestrainedly as they lounged about the white and gold settees.

All of them were clad most magnificently, and outrivaled in their costumes the creations which the ladies wore.

" 'Tis—'tis-a mighty pity that Lady Gug-gug-Gloria hath banned the c-c-cards," said Sir Brian

Bushworthy, who lay stretched out on a settee with most doleful expression on his countenance.

Sir Rupert sighed.

"Faith, you're right for once, Bushie. But it's the outcome o' that duel that was fought by Anderley—that is—I mean by the man who called himself Anderley."

Sir Brian looked at him.

"Hast s-s-een the n-notice Sir Humphrey hath p-p-posted at the g-gate?" he stuttered.

Sir Rupert nodded.

"Aye," he said slowly. "It offers a hundred guineas reward for the capture of this man Shale, dead or alive."

There was a long pause. Then Sir Rupert continued:

"I doubt me if I'd tell Sir Humphrey where he was, even if I knew. He was a fine fellow, that man Shale—even if he was an impostor."

"And a m-m-murderer," put in Sir Brian. "D-d'ye remember how he c-c-could f-fence?"

"Aye. He was the finest blade I've seen, and, look you, friend Bushie, beware how you speak o' him 'fore Lady Gloria. Art such a fool, man, as not to see that she is sorely saddened by this strange turn o' affairs?"

He sighed, and looked over to where Gloria

sat on a stool before the fire, staring into the center of the ruddy flames.

Her golden hair glistened in the leaping red light, but there was a wistful sadness about her face.

Sometimes her lip seemed to quiver a little, but always she regained command of it and strove to keep it still.

The other women were paying but little attention to her. They were absorbed in excited discussion of the death of Lord Anderley, and the remarkable imposture by this man Shale.

The door was thrust open, and Sir Humphrey stamped into the room. His face was flushed with much wine that he had consumed, but withal he seemed mightily well pleased with himself.

"Gad, Gloria," he roared, "what's the matter with you? Why sit so doleful there when our guests need entertainment? You've banned the cards, girl, so 'tis for you to supply other entertainment."

She rose wearily to her feet.

"I feel in no mood for merriment—uncle," she replied in a low voice. "'Tis surely right to honor the death of our neighbor, Lord Anderley, by maintaining more subdued mien to-night."

Sir Humphrey let out a string of oaths, regardless, as he always was, of the presence of ladies.

" 'Tis not for Lord Anderley you grieve, girl," he roared. "I know full well. You never met him in your life—'tis for that blackguard who hath gulled us these past few days that you pine—e'en though he is a—a murderer."

A sudden silence fell upon the company. Lady Gloria was deathly pale, and she swayed as if to fall; but she recovered herself and raised her head proudly, though she uttered no word.

Sir Rupert pushed forward.

"Faith, Sir Humphrey, keep a better hold on that tongue o' yours, or, though I'm your guest, I yet may be forced to teach you manners."

Sir Humphrey went purple, but, knowing Sir Rupert's swordsmanship, he contented himself with merely swearing harder than ever.

Gloria gave him one contemptuous glance, then turned to Sir Rupert.

"Your arm, Sir Rupert," she said. "I would have you lead me to the ante-room where I may rest upon a couch. I feel me faint and deep oppressed by the heat o' this room."

He bowed, and gracefully offered her his arm, and thus they passed in silence from the room.

When they had gone Sir Humphrey stamped around, somewhat in the nature of a triumphal march, offering pinches of snuff to the men and grinning banefully at the ladies, who simpered before him.

"Found out who that impostor was as neatly as the best Bow Street runner could have done," he announced. "Fellow named Shale, he is. Used to be a farmer on one o' my estates, but my bailiffs turned him out. Demmed wise thing to do, too."

"Law, Sir Humphrey, but you are clever," simpered Sir Brian Bushworthy's spouse. "If only Brian had half your brain."

Sir Humphrey bowed, but Sir Brian spluttered furiously.

"H-he did-didn't find out at-at all," he gasped out. "One of his m-m-men h-heard the l-l-landlord of the 'Why-Whyte Hart' tell L-Lady Gloria t-that he'd seen Sh-Shale and Lord Anderley to-to-to-together."

"Grr," growled Sir Humphrey. "Demme, man, 'twas I sent my fellow to the 'Whyte Hart' to find out why Lady Gloria went there."

Sir Brian turned on him.

"Th-then you spied upon—your own n-n-niece."

Sir Humphrey flushed again, and tried to cover his embarrassment by burying his face in his hand while he took a tremendous pinch of snuff.

"No matter," he roared. "I found out who

he was, and that's enough. Aye, and what's more, I've posted to-night a notice at my gate to tell the countryside to look out for this murderer."

"Beware he d-doesn't look out f-for you," retorted Sir Brian.

Sir Humphrey laughed boastfully, and struck his chest.

"Me!" he shouted. "Think you that I am afraid of a low-down farmer. Faith, an I had him here now I'd clap him in irons beside that man Peter o' his, who now lies in my cellar, for 'tis plain he must have known o' the murder and imposture."

"An' he were here you'd make but a poor show," said Sir Brian scornfully.

Sir Humphrey stamped in fury.

"We'll see," he roared. "We'll see—wait till I get him—I'll show you what——"

A mighty crash sounded outside in the hall, then a hoarse shout rang out.

A footman dashed into the room. His face was deathly white.

"Master! master!" he shouted, "there's a madman—a madman coming."

He stopped abruptly as another crash rang out.

The eyes of the whole company turned towards the door.

A sound of heavy footsteps, of panting breath —then a gasp of horror from Sir Humphrey.

There, in the doorway, loomed up a strange figure of a man.

His face was covered with blood—his hair tangled and tossed—his eyes blazed with a fierce glare—his clothes were in tatters, and an ugly wound showed in his left arm where his sleeve was rent open. His great shoulders towered in the doorway, and—strangest of all—in his hands, uplifted in the air like a huge unwieldy battle-axe, was the signpost and board which but a few moments before had stood at the gate of Clayville Grange.

"My God!" gasped Sir Brian. "Shale!"

LADY GLORIA SAVES A LIFE

A TENSE silence fell upon the company.
All eyes were fixed upon the strange wild figure in the doorway.

Sir Humphrey's face blanched. He swayed as if to fall, but steadied himself by clutching hold of the back of a chair.

There was a low, ominous growl, and the man at the door moved forward.

With an effort Sir Humphrey found his voice.

"Who are you?" he cried. "Speak, who are you?"

A hoarse, gruesome laugh burst from the man.

"Who am I?" boomed his powerful voice. "Dost not know me—look at my face. Who am I—but——"

He paused.

"Aye, who?" cried Sir Humphrey, backing away.

A fierce exultant roar greeted him.

"I am Lord Anderley!"

Sir Humphrey stared, and his whiteness turned to a sickly green. Sir Brian spluttered and rubbed his eyes.

Again that raucous laugh rang out.

"Aye, look at me, Sir Humphrey Clayville— look at me full and fair. Gaze upon my face and say who I am."

Sir Humphrey looked around in terror at the others of the company.

"Keep close by me, gentlemen," his voice, now very weak, pleaded. "He is mad. He might do me harm."

A gust of passion seemed to sweep across the face of the intruder, leaving it livid and contorted with fury.

"Do you harm? Aye, you've said it—and not all the swordsmen in England can save you. You have called me murderer—but you have lied. To-night I am only executioner. You are the murderer, and well you know it."

He took another step towards the quaking wretch, and his mighty wooden axe was raised to strike.

"Help me—help me," cried Sir Humphrey.

At last the gallants recovered their senses, and with hoarse cries drew their swords.

But the fury in the avenger's face made them shudder.

"Back, dogs! Back!" he roared, swinging the great post in a mighty sweep that forced them to recoil quickly. "Back to your kennels—while I slay this vile assassin."

Sir Brian alone found his voice.

"Stay, man. Why do you do this?" he burst out, without even the semblance of a stutter. "Are you not John Shale?"

The man paused in his mad career for a second.

"Aye, that was my name, but now—I am Lord Anderley. Stand back—stand back, for this is the moment of death for that fiend."

With a mighty heave he raised the huge sign-post high above his head, and lurched towards Sir Humphrey.

Gasps of horror broke from the helpless watchers. The women fainted, and even the men closed their eyes to shut out the sight of that mighty wooden club crashing down upon the skull of Clayville.

'Twas a moment of dire suspense.

Then a strange thing happened.

There was a cry of terror in girlish tone, and the blue and gold curtain that cut off the ante-room was pulled quickly aside.

John Shale's eyes left Sir Humphrey's bloated

visage, and rising, fell upon the face of the girl who stood before the curtain.

He stared at her, and as he did so he swayed unsteadily.

He seemed to forget all else save that she was there—that the Lady Gloria was watching him.

The great signpost faltered in its death-dealing course as his nerveless fingers relaxed their grip upon it.

With a resounding, splintering crash, it fell heavily to the ground, missing Sir Humphrey by merely a few inches.

The noise seemed to rouse the men in the room to fresh action, and several of them ran forward towards Shale with drawn swords.

But he seemed neither to see nor heed them. His eyes were fixed in dazed, helpless fashion upon Gloria.

Then suddenly he put his hands to his face as if to shut out the sight of her, and stood thus blinded at their mercy.

Sir Humphrey gave a fierce oath, and rushed forward to plunge his rapier into Shale's heart. But ere he could reach him, Sir Rupert's own blade had struck his up.

"Back, back," cried Sir Rupert. "Would'st strike the man who spared you?"

Sir Humphrey paused, glaring furiously at Shale.

The latter swayed where he stood, then slowly —very, very slowly—he took his hands from his face and raised his head.

Now the glare of fury had departed from his eyes, and in its place was that cold, steely expressionless look which all who had seen him had linked with the Lord Anderley they knew.

He raised his head almost proudly, and running his fingers through his crisp hair relieved somewhat its entanglement, making him look less fierce.

The blood was still streaked across his face, but somehow it did not seem so terrible as before.

His hand reached out and touched Sir Rupert's shoulder.

"Stand aside, friend," he said, "lest you come to harm. You are but one against many."

Sir Rupert stared at him in amazement, and, indeed, so overcome was he that he forgot about Sir Humphrey and the others, and before he could recover himself they were upon him.

At the same instant three footmen, who had rushed into the room, seized Shale from behind, grappling with him fiercely.

To their huge surprise, however, he made no

attempt to resist them, but stood grimly silent with bowed head and almost humble mien.

Seeing this, Sir Humphrey stamped around him triumphantly.

"Tie up his hands," he roared. "Put chains upon the dog and throw him into the cellar. He'll hang for this night's work alone."

Shale raised his head, and gazed dumbly at Lady Gloria.

Her eyes were upon him, staring in sheer bewilderment. Was this the man who, but a moment before, had bound that throng in a spell of terror? Was this humble, helpless soul the awe-inspiring figure she had seen when, attracted by the noise, she had pulled aside the curtains from the ante-room?

Slowly she advanced and stood before him.

"Why—why have you come here?" she asked in a low, quivering voice.

His face twitched, and he looked towards the signpost lying broken upon the floor. His lips moved, and he spoke scarcely above a whisper.

"It—it called me MURDERER!"

She looked at him a long time, till the tears that rushed to her eyes blinded her so that she could not see his face, and only saw, through the haze, the blood upon it.

A dead silence filled the room. Every one

seemed afraid even to breathe. Tragedy and mystery hovered in the air.

Suddenly, in the very midst of that grim silence, a queer tapping sound was heard.

There it was again. "Tap—tap—tap—tap—tap."

It seemed to come from the half-open case-ment, and now all slowly turned and looked towards it.

Without warning one of the women shrieked.

The casement was opening slowly—very slowly—so slowly as to be hardly perceptible in its movement. Yet there was no doubting the fact—it was opening.

With a low oath Sir Rupert leaped forward towards it and pulled it wide apart.

As he did so there was a heavy thud, and the body of a man fell upon the floor.

In an instant all was commotion. The women who had just recovered from their fainting fits promptly screamed and went off into them again. The men were too excited to catch them in their arms, and so these ladies perforce had to maneuver their passage into unconsciousness so that they fell upon the soft cushions of the settee —which they did with truly wonderful adroit-ness.

The footmen still clung to Shale, but he, like

the others, was looking at the man who had
fallen upon the floor.

He lay, face downwards, panting heavily and
seeming too exhausted to raise himself up.

He was a fat man—and, moreover, a little
man. His clothes were very tattered, and covered with mud, as if he had crawled some
distance along the ground.

"Gad, what's here now?" muttered Sir Rupert.
"Are we never to be free from scares this
night?"

" 'T-'tis one f-fight after another," quoth Sir
Brian. "My w-w-wife has fainted four t-t-times
already, and n-n-now she is off a-again, th-thank
g-goodness."

"For shame, Sir Brian," cried Gloria, pushing
him aside. "To make a joke o' such affair as
this. Dost not see the man is bleeding from a
wound in his side?"

Sir Brian's wife, opening her eyes at the sound
of her husband's voice, promptly screamed and
passed once more into oblivion.

"Turn him over," ordered Sir Humphrey
gruffly. "We'll see what the dog wants here."

Sir Rupert stooped and raised the man's
head up.

Sir Humphrey leaned forward and gazed into
his face, then sprank back with a sudden oath.

"Why, it's Benjamin Greenleaf," he burst out. "What want you, man? Dost know you have no right within my house?"

At the sound of bullying tones, the fellow's eyes opened and slowly he looked around the company, first at Shale, who stood with a grim smile upon his lips, then at the circle of gallants and the ladies lying in their swoons—then, lastly, at Sir Humphrey Clayville.

For a long time he stared at the latter, till the knight began to move uneasily.

"Well, man, speak if you can. What do you want?"

A wry smile twisted itself upon the pallid lips of the little fat man.

" 'Tis—little—wonder—an' I cannot speak," he muttered aloud. "And no fault of yours, master."

A curse broke from Sir Humphrey.

"What mean you?" he demanded, in a thick voice.

Benjamin with a mighty effort raised his hand and pointed at him.

"There stands the murderer of Lord Anderley," he cried excitedly. "He paid Simon Grappletight and I to do the deed—but, as God is my judge, 'twas Simon who shot him. And, moreover, he shot me, too, this very night, at Sir Humphrey's command."

Sir Humphrey swung round in terrified fury.

" 'Tis false," he roared. "He lies. 'Twas Shale who killed Lord Anderley."

Again that silent, ominous smile played across Benjamin's face.

"Look—look you within my pocket," he gasped to Sir Rupert. "There you will find a parchment giving Simon and I protection should we be accused o' the murder of Lord Anderley. 'Tis signed by Sir Humphrey Clayville."

He fell back exhausted, and now all eyes turned upon the master of Clayville Grange.

His usually purple visage had turned a greeny-white. Cold sweat-drops stood out upon his forehead, and his hands shook as if palsied.

For a moment he looked fearfully about him like a hunted hare in a trap; then suddenly, ere any one could intervene, he swung himself around and dashed headlong through the casement, banging it fiercely behind him.

For a moment no one moved except Sir Rupert, who thrust his hand into the pocket of Benjamin's jerkin and withdrew from it a piece of soiled parchment.

Seeing this, Sir Bushworthy gave a shout and rushed towards the window.

"After him," he cried. "He is t-t-trying to escape because he is g-g-guilty."

The other men seemed to realize the full import of his words at last, and with hoarse cries and much brandishing of swords they dashed out into the blackness of the night.

PRINCIPALLY DEALS WITH THE SPEAKING OF A
LADY'S NAME

SHALE, with a mighty wrench, shook himself
free of his captors.

The three footmen reeled across the room, and,
when they could recover themselves, stood staring at him as though chary of risking their skins
by open attack. Lady Gloria turned to them.

"You may go," she commanded. "All of you."

They slunk gratefully from the room like
whipped dogs with tails 'tween legs.

Sir Rupert handed Gloria the slip of parchment he had taken from the pocket of the
wounded man who lay back breathing heavily.
She read it through almost wearily, then bowed
her head.

" 'Tis plain my uncle didst instigate the
crime," she said, her face very pale. "Yet I hope
that he—is not caught. 'Twould nigh kill me
with the very shame o't."

She turned at the sound of a heavy step.

Shale was walking slowly through the doorway. His head hung forward heavily upon his breast, and his feet somehow seemed to drag.

She hastened forward and touched him on the arm.

He stopped outside the door and, turning, looked down at her. Now the expression upon his face was most tender, though in truth the streak of blood sadly spoiled the effect.

Her lips moved.

"M'lord!"

He smiled a wan smile.

"Aye, m'lady."

The tears blinded her eyes, but she gazed upwards at him bravely.

"Art thou truly m'lord?"

"If so you mean that I am Lord Anderley— aye, m'lady."

A sob.

" 'Tis passing strange, m'lord."

He bowed his head.

"Aye, m'lady, 'tis passing strange."

She looked away.

"I—I—thought after you had—had gone— that you must—must be the real Lord Anderley, after all," she said. "There was your fencing, the trick you said was your greatest heritage, and I remembered that Aunt Genevieve did inform me how her sister had fled from the

French court with a fencing master who had won her love. That if she bore a son, he would be heir to Anderley."

The tender expression deepened in his eyes.

"She—she was my—mother," he said very softly.

There was a long silence, then she spoke again.

"And did you know all the time?" she asked.

He shook his head.

"Nay, m'lady. I did not know till I saw a portrait of my mother in the gallery at Anderley Hall. 'Twas the same as a miniature I carry in this locket round my neck. It never leaves me."

He thrust his hand in the neck of his tattered shirt, and withdrew a golden locket. On it were the arms and crest of the Anderleys. He pressed it open, and showed her the tiny portrait of a most beautiful woman.

She looked at it with something akin to wonder.

"I know it," she said. "Aunt Genevieve told me that her sister took it with her when she—she eloped."

He smiled grimly, then with a sudden jerk he broke the gold chain, and held the locket out to her.

She looked up at him in strange bewilderment.

"Why—why," she gasped.

"Take it," he muttered. "It has never left me before, but now—I would ask you to keep it for me, and mayhap to treasure it."

She took it tenderly, and stood gazing down upon it lying within the hollow of her hand.

While she was thus engaged, Shale silently turned away, and moved a-down the corridor.

She sensed that he was leaving her, but was afraid to raise her head since the tears blinded her so.

"M'lord," she whispered.

He paused again, but did not look around.

"Where do you go, m'lord?"

A long silence. Then:

"I go—where I go, m'lady—and that is where the white road leads me."

Something in the nature of a sob broke from her.

"Ah, m'lord, m'lord, but why do you go?"

"To forget an' I can that I e'er was so dishonorable as to take another's name."

Again that sob.

"E'en though 'twere your own name, m'lord?"

"Aye, for the intention to sin was there."

She went towards him again, and now he felt her hand quivering upon his arm.

"Ah, then, m'lord—is it thus you do your duty?"

He looked at her in wide amaze.

"My duty, m'lady. Alas! it is but penance I would do."

"And what o' me, m'lord?"

Something tight seemed to grip his heart.

"I—I cannot understand. Prithee, tell me what mean you, m'lady?"

Again she sighed.

"Faith, you disappoint me mightily, m'lord. I had thought you were most shrewd of wit. Know you not that this house and these lands around it are my sole heritage."

He looked down at her in wonderment.

"Aye, m'lady, but—but an' I be dense I fail me to grasp your meaning."

She raised her head, and now he saw a strange light shining in her eyes. It made him draw his breath quickly. It was a light that seemed to breathe forth love, and set his heart a-beating very fast.

"M'lady, m'lady," he said, as in a dream, his hands rising to her shoulders to touch her, as if she were a sacred thing.

"Aye, m'lord," she whispered softly—her eyes dimmed afresh with sudden tears.

"I—I think, m'lady, I am not yet so dull of wit as you would make me out."

She bowed her head demurely. And now he

found that he was gazing a-down upon these golden curls that glistened so entrancingly in the candle-light.

"M'lady," he said again.

"Aye, m'lord."

He took a deep breath, then:

"An' you marry not Lord Anderley, you lose these lands."

Her answer came very, very softly.

"M'lord, you are truly wise."

He folded his arms about her, and to his vast amaze she did not resist him.

"M'lady," he whispered. " 'Twas for these lands I took another's name. So now for them wilt thou take mine?"

A soft sob, half muffled by his shoulder, came from her.

"Nay, nay, m'lord."

He drew back quickly, and looking down at her, sighed deep.

"Ah, then my wit most truly hath deserted me," he muttered in despondency.

She raised her face to his.

"Indeed it hath, m'lord. For 'tis not for lands alone that I would take thy name, but——"

"Ah, m'lady, ah. I pray thee proceed."

Again her face was hidden and her voice was

muffled, but stooping above her he heard the wondrous words:

"For love, m'lord."

And then at last he did breathe her name.

"Gloria."

So for a long, long time there was silence— golden silence.

BENJAMIN REMEMBERS HIS KNACK O' JANGLING WORDS

THE Lady Gloria and John Shale entered the drawing-room to find that Sir Rupert had lifted little Benjamin on to a couch, and was busily engaged stopping the flow of blood from the wound in his side.

The baronet looked up as they entered.

"Egad! Shale, 'tis time you had a wash up," he laughed; "you look as if you had been fighting a regiment and, faith, so you very nearly did, in sooth."

Shale looked at himself in the mantel mirror and, observing the blood upon his face and the muddy and tattered condition of his clothes, he stared in amaze.

"Gad!" he muttered. "I am indeed a sorry sight. And these are all the garments I possess. Here's a pretty pickle for a man to be in."

Lady Gloria looked at him tenderly.

"Nay, m'lord. Have you forgotten already that you are Lord Anderley, and that no more need you wear these homespun garments, or even that—that tall, furry hat, which I have treasured me these few days."

Shale gave a sigh of relief.

"Ah, yes, of course," he said. "Once more I will parade myself about my estates in silken breeches and satin coat—though, in truth, I shall be sorry to part with these old rags. They have served me well."

Sir Rupert was looking at him curiously.

"So you are actually the real heir to Anderley," he said. "Faith, 'twas plain that most 'mazing likeness to—to the other must bear a blood relationship. So you are the true son of the Lady Anderley and the fencing master who was the lion of the French court thirty years ago. I've heard my father speak o' his wonderful power wi' the blade."

Shale bowed his head.

"Aye, I am his son," he said in a low voice.

Sir Rupert turned to Lady Gloria.

"Faith, you'd better despatch a messenger posthaste to the Lady Genevieve to tell her the good news," he said. "Though I'll warrant me she knew who the heir to Anderley Hall was all the time. 'Tis ever her way to be prepared for emergencies."

Gloria smiled.

"In truth, it takes much to rouse Aunt

Genevieve," she said, "but I think this news will make her most excited."

She turned and, ringing a bell, ordered a footman to send a courier to Anderley Hall to tell the Lady Genevieve that the son of her sister and the new heir to Anderley had been found, and his name was John Shale.

While she was speaking to the footman, little Benjamin opened his eyes and stared at Shale.

"Gad!" he muttered. "So you are Lord Anderley, after all? 'Tis more than my poor brain can understand. First Simon doth shoot Anderley, then Anderley doth pose as Anderley, and I am haunted by Anderley, while at the same time I do tell Anderley that he is accused o' killing Anderley. Faith, 'tis a puzzle."

Shale and Sir Rupert laughed heartily.

"Ah, Benjamin," quoth the former, "I see you still have the knack of jangling words and phrases, most entertaining."

Benjamin made a grimace.

"Faith, m'lord, Simon Grappletight nigh chased that knack out o' my system with an ounce o' lead."

"Where did you encounter him," asked Shale curiously.

"In the garden, m'lord. When you did chase me in the woods I hied me to the Grange to see

if you would really come here, and, faith, when
I arrived at the gate and looked me for the signpost which had stood there, I could scarce believe
my eyes, for it was gone, and nothing but the
splintered stump of it was left. So I did pursue
my investigations further, and entered me the
grounds of the Grange. I was crossing the lawn
near the old hunting box when I encountered
Simon."

"Aye, go on," sighed Shale, watching him
intently, as indeed were also the Lady Gloria
and Sir Rupert.

"Well, Simon he greeted me with much abuse,"
went on the little man. "And he swore most
solemnly that an' I moved a foot towards the
house he would pump me full of lead. So,
knowing Simon, I did believe him and hastily
withdrew my carcass to the thicket beyond the
lawn, there to watch my chance to reach the
house unharmed. Accordingly, after some few
minutes, I essayed me another attempt, and once
more I did encounter Simon, who did not wait
to threaten, but pulled the trigger of his pistol
and winged me in the side. Then he departed
as quickly as his legs could carry him, leaving
me for dead. And for myself I believed that I
was dying and, though I am not over righteous,
I deemed it unwise to enter the next world with-

out denouncing Simon, and so struggled across the lawn to the window there and tapped upon it in the fashion you know."

Shale crossed to him and took his hand.

"You have done well, Benjamin Greenleaf," he said, "and I shall remember it ever."

"Faith, so shall I," grinned the little man, "and master, an' you'd be grateful, wilt do me a favor?"

"Say it, and it is done," said Shale.

"Well, master, there's that flagon of brandy on the table. Now, I am a sick man, m'lord, mighty sorely wounded and methinks 'tis most providential that yon decanter should be there now——"

Amidst much laughter, Sir Rupert reached for the brandy, and pouring out a stiff glass passed it to Benjamin.

Suddenly Gloria spoke.

"M'lord—your arm, it is bleeding most grievously from that wound Sir Claude Aylesbury gave you."

Shale looked down at it.

" 'Tis nothing but a scratch," he said, then added quickly, "m'lady, hast any notion where that—that knave, Peter, hath gotten to?"

Gloria started and bit her lips at her forgetfulness.

"Why, poor fellow, he is in the cellar," she announced.

"In the cellar," he repeated wonderingly. "What does he there?"

She smiled tenderly up at him.

"Why, m'lord, he—he was imprisoned there by Sir Humphrey, who said he was an accomplice of—of——"

She paused.

"Aye, go on, m'lady."

"Of yours, m'lord."

Shale laughed heartily.

"Ah, well, suppose we visit the vault and see how he hath been conducting himself," he suggested.

Gloria smiled roguishly.

"Why, yes, m'lord, methinks 'tis time he were released and, moreover, I suspect me he will be most grievously upset pondering o'er your fate. 'Twas always plain he had a strange liking for you, m'lord."

Shale laughed.

" 'Tis one of these unaccountable things, m'lady. I cannot understand any one having a liking for such a dolesome wretch as I, yet, m'lady, it gives me new heart to think that there are one or two who do regard me in somewhat friendly fashion."

She lowered her eyes demurely.

"Did'st say friendly, m'lord?" she murmured.

He looked at her.

"Aye, m'lady, but—but methinks 'twas for want of a better word. There is one such word, but 'tis seldom spoken of in company."

He wagged his head jocularly at Sir Rupert.

The latter drew himself up in mock disdain.

"Truly, m'lord, the setting of a scene is nigh as important as the scene itself. Pray, do not let me keep you from—your cellar."

Gloria blushed furiously, and Shale laughed heartily.

" 'Tis good advice, Sir Rupert," he said— "m'lady, wilt lean you on this fearsome-looking arm o' mine?"

She took it gently.

"Nay, m'lord, I will but hold it thus that you may not feel the pain o't so intense."

She dropped a pretty curtsey to Sir Rupert, and then looked up at John Shale with happy tears shining in her eyes.

"M'lord. 'Tis this way to—to the—cellar."

M'LADY FORGETS HOW TO WEEP

'TWAS midsummer.

Bright, warm sunshine streamed down from the blue skies. It broke through the flower-covered walk leading to the pretty little bower in the rose garden at Anderley Hall.

All the flowers in the garden were a-bloom, and raised their petaled heads high in the breathless air, sending forth their sweet scent far and wide for all live things to inhale.

Big bees from the hives and woods lingered amongst the flowers and their soft dreamy drone, with the chirping of the birds like the deep base of an organ accompanying the treble notes.

Right in front of the rose bower stood a man gazing silently down at it. He was a tall man with handsome face, somewhat serious, though lightened at the moment by a tender smile.

He was dressed in immaculate silk knee breeches and brocaded coat, with white hose and silver-buckled shoon.

A gold laced three-cornered hat was on his

head, but at the back there showed his crisp black curly hair.

He stood thus musing so unconsciously that he did not hear light footsteps tripping down the covered walk until the girl was close behind him. Then with a start and a glad smile he turned round.

She looked up at him.

"Why, John, dear, whatever were you standing staring at," she cried merrily.

He stooped and tenderly kissed her.

" 'Twas nothing, dear m'lady," he murmured. " 'Twas nothing."

She stood back and waggled a tiny forefinger at him in roguish fashion.

"M'lord Anderley, you are not telling me the truth."

He laughed.

"Nay, M'lady Anderley. In very sooth, I was but looking at—at yonder pretty roses in the bower."

She pouted.

"But why at them, when there are so many more beautiful in the garden?"

He sighed deeply.

"In—in truth, m'lady, 'twas but a small matter —a most unimportant personal affair."

Again she pouted.

"So you have secrets from your wife, m'lord."

He hastily tried to retrieve his position.

"Nay, nay, dear m'lady," he said desperately. "I pray you believe me, I was but looking——"

He stopped and then gave a light, little laugh as he caught the merry gleam in her eyes.

"Well, m'lord?" she demanded.

He put his arm about her.

"You know full well, you little witch," he said, gazing deep down into her eyes. "I was but looking at——"

"Aye, John dear, aye," she breathed.

He kissed her hair.

"I was but looking at the spot where once I caught a maid a-weeping because she was betrothed to my very self."

She laid her head upon his shoulder with a sigh of content.

"Ah, John. She was a very foolish maid, but she hath truly learned much since then, and hath, I fear, well nigh forgotten how to weep."

Whereupon a pearly tear trickled a-down her cheek, and stained somewhat the satin o' Lord Anderley's new coat.

'Twas thus that Master Peter Cherryblossom found them, and immediately he had visioned them he stopped in his walk and tip-toed out of earshot with elaborate care, lest the rattle of a pebble should disturb their peace.   And when he had put a safe distance between them, he produced him a huge red kerchief and, after first casting a wary glance around him to insure his secrecy, he wiped his honest eyes and blew his nose with much trumpeting.

When he had recovered his dignity, he turned and looked towards the spot where the rose-covered bower was.

"Now, I wonder what that old villain, Sir Humphrey, would say an' he could see them now, bless 'em," he muttered to himself. "Peter, m'lad, if on'y you hadn't been locked up in that there cellar when m'lord came back to his heritage, and said good-by to the white road, you would have made certain sure the rascal didn't escape.   I suppose he and yon knave, Simon, have shook the dust o' Kent from their feet ere now, and i'faith 'tis much to Kent's advantage."

He sighed, and turned towards the house.

Now, as he did so, there arose upon the still summer air, the faint sound of a man a-singing in the distance, and the song that he sang was worded after this fashion:

> My Polly's hair is like the flare,
> That marks the leaping flame.

My Polly's eyes are like the skies:
    Their color is the same.
Ah, you should see my Polly's feet,
There's none in County Kent so neat,
Nor is there e'en a wife so sweet,
    And Polly is her name.

Cheer-o, cheer-o, but I'm a merry wight,
    A-grooming horses all day long,
    And singing of my gleesome song
That makes me feel more bright,
Aye, that makes me feel more bright.

The hearing which, Peter did blow his nose
again most fiercely, and did mutter—"Zookers!"

(1)

THE END

www.ingramcontent.com/pod-product-compliance
Lightning Source LLC
Chambersburg PA
CBHW020643030726
47498CB00002B/345